"Any sign of the men or the hostages?"

"None." Josh put down his hands but didn't move off the bed. He stayed right there looming over her.

And he was naked.

Jaycee did a double take.

Okay, not naked. Just shirtless.

She had a good view of not just those toned abs and pecs but also the scar. It was several inches long and gashed across his otherwise perfect body. Even though it was well healed, she figured the ashy white line would never go away.

The memory of it certainly wouldn't.

JOSH

USA TODAY Bestselling Author
DELORES FOSSEN

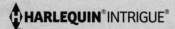

Recycling programs
for this product may
not exist in your area.

ISBN-13: 978-0-373-69752-6

JOSH

HARLEQUIN®
www.Harlequin.com

Printed in U.S.A.

ABOUT THE AUTHOR

Imagine a family tree that includes Texas cowboys, Choctaw and Cherokee Indians, a Louisiana pirate and a Scottish rebel who battled side by side with William Wallace. With ancestors like that, it's easy to understand why *USA TODAY* bestselling author and former air force captain Delores Fossen feels as if she were genetically predisposed to writing romances. Along the way to fulfilling her DNA destiny, Delores married an air force top gun who just happens to be of Viking descent. With all those romantic bases covered, she doesn't have to look too far for inspiration.

Books by Delores Fossen

HARLEQUIN INTRIGUE

CAST OF CHARACTERS

Deputy Josh Ryland—A former FBI agent recovering from a near-fatal attack. He returns home to Silver Creek looking for a quieter life but encounters an old flame who's not only pregnant, but also in grave danger.

Jaycee Finney—Kidnapped and held captive, she must rely on Josh, the man who nearly died because of her rogue investigation.

Bryson Hills—Businessman in need of an heir to collect his inheritance. Just how far would he go to have a child?

Valeria DeSilva—A prominent attorney who's handled many adoptions. She might be involved in a dangerous but lucrative black-market baby ring.

Sierra DeSilva—A pregnant gold digger who claims she's been held captive by someone who planned to sell her baby.

Miranda Culley—The authorities are looking for her because she might have answers about the babies being sold and illegally adopted.

Sheriff Grayson Ryland—The sheriff of Silver Creek, and Josh's boss

Chapter One

This was exactly the kind of *homecoming* that Deputy Josh Ryland had wanted to avoid.

Just the sight of the guy with the gun caused his head to start pounding, and his heartbeat crashed in his ears. The flashbacks came.

Man, did they.

Flashbacks of another surveillance, another gunman. And the three .38 jacketed slugs that the gunman had fired into Josh's chest. The wounds had healed, for the most part anyway, but still the flashbacks came.

"You okay?" his cousin whispered.

His cousin was Grayson Ryland, sheriff of Silver Creek, Josh's hometown where he'd been born and had spent his childhood. Not a town where Josh had expected to see a man carrying an assault rifle. It wasn't exactly a standard weapon for a Texas cattle rancher.

"I'm fine," Josh lied. And he tried to level his breathing. Tried also to ignore the healing gunshot wounds on his chest that had started to throb like a bad toothache.

"I can call one of the other deputies to come out here," Grayson offered.

There was no shortage of them. Like Grayson, four of the deputies were Josh's cousins, too. And if Grayson had thought for one second that he would encounter a rifle-toting man on what should have been a routine call, then he would have almost certainly brought one of the others and not Josh.

"You made me a deputy," Josh reminded him. "This is part of the job."

That sounded good. Like something a small-town deputy should say to his boss.

It was pretty much a lie, though.

The truth was, Josh had come back home after taking a leave of absence from the FBI so he could avoid gunmen. Assault rifles. Bullets to the chest. And the tangle of bloody memories that he fought hard to keep out of his head.

So much for that plan.

Using the binoculars, Josh watched the rifleman pace across the front porch of the two-story ranch house. He was clearly standing guard.

But why?

Too bad Josh could think of several reasons why a rancher would need a guard with an assault rifle, and none of those reasons involved anything legal.

Josh handed Grayson the binoculars so he, too, could have a look. "You think they're hiding drugs in the house?" Grayson asked.

"Drugs or guns, maybe."

Whichever it was, it had created a lot of traffic, because there were plenty of tire tracks on the gravel driveway in front of the ranch house.

It was that unusual traffic that had prompted someone to make an anonymous call to the sheriff's office to report possible suspicious activity at the ranch. It didn't help that no one knew the tenants. The place had recently been rented by a couple from nearby San Antonio who'd yet to turn up in town.

Josh could see the source of some of that traffic. There were four vehicles—two trucks, an SUV and a car, all parked around the grounds. No tractors, no livestock or any signs of any ranching equipment.

That didn't help the knot in Josh's stomach.

"The gunman's not the new tenant of the place," Grayson explained.

No. Josh had glanced at the couple's driver's license photos in the background info that he'd pulled up on them before Grayson and he had even started the half-hour drive from Silver Creek out to the Bluebonnet Ranch. A peaceful-sounding name for a place that was probably hiding some very unpeaceful secrets.

And speaking of hiding, the front door of the ranch house flew open, and Josh didn't need the binoculars to see another armed man step into the doorway.

Yeah, this was definitely a bad homecoming.

Grayson and he stayed belly down on the side of the hill dotted with spring wildflowers that overlooked the ranch, and Grayson returned the binoculars to Josh so he could take out his phone and call for backup. Unfortunately, they were going to need it.

Josh zoomed in on the second guard who'd stepped onto the porch. Both men were dressed in dark clothes, and both carried the same type of assault rifle. Maybe they were part of a militia group, though Josh hadn't heard of any reports of that kind of activity in Silver Creek.

The second man glanced around. The kind of glance that a cop or criminal would make to ensure he wasn't being watched. Josh was pretty certain that Grayson and he were well hidden, but he ducked down lower just in case, and he watched the man motion toward someone else in the doorway.

A woman stepped out.

And Josh's pulse kicked up a significant notch.

He adjusted the zoom on the binoculars. Hoping he was wrong. But he wasn't.

Josh instantly recognized that pale blond hair. That face. Even the body that was hidden beneath a bulky pair of green scrubs and a gray windbreaker.

Jaycee.

Last time he'd seen Jaycee Finney was the morning of his shooting when she'd been half-naked and skulking out of his bedroom. He hadn't stopped her, that was for sure, because he'd already figured out that a weekend affair with a fellow agent was a bad idea. After the shooting and after he'd realized what she'd done, Josh knew it hadn't been just bad. It had been one of the worst mistakes of his life.

"You know her?" Grayson whispered when he finished his call for backup.

Obviously, something in Josh's body language had clued Grayson in to that possibility. Probably the narrowed eyes or the veins that Josh could feel pulsing on his forehead.

"Yeah. She's Special Agent Jaycee Finney." And if Jaycee was here, that meant the FBI was already aware of something illegal taking place on the ranch.

Josh took out his phone and called his brother, Sawyer, who was an FBI agent in the San Antonio office. "You ready to come back to work, little brother?" Sawyer said the moment he answered.

"Not exactly. Fill me in on SA Jaycee Finney."

Unlike his cheerful greeting, Sawyer didn't jump to answer that, cheerful or otherwise, but Josh heard what sounded like keystrokes on a computer.

"Please tell me you're not involved with her again," Sawyer implored.

"Not like *that*."

"Good. Because she's bad news."

Oh, yeah. No arguments from him on that.

Josh had learned his lesson when it came to Jaycee. She would do any- and everything for the badge, and while Josh had once put himself in that same super-troop category, he never would have risked another lawman's life.

As Jaycee had done.

Josh kept his attention fastened to her and watched as the second gunman grabbed her by the arm. She didn't fight back, though he knew she was capable of it. She didn't appear to be armed, either. Jaycee just let the goon practically drag her off the porch and into the yard.

Even though Jaycee and he didn't have a good history together, it still took everything inside him to stay put and not bolt out there to help a fellow law enforcement agent. This was obviously some deep-cover assignment, and playing knight in shining armor could get her killed. Grayson, too.

"Seems like you're not the only one who wanted some downtime," Sawyer finally said. "I just checked the computer, and it says Jaycee's been on a leave of absence for nearly four months now."

That didn't mesh with what was playing out in front of him. Either Jaycee was doing her own rogue private investigation or else she'd been taken captive.

Josh watched as the guard shoved her in the direction of a barn that was almost the same size as the house. "Any ransom demands for her?" he asked Sawyer.

"Ransom? None. Why? What in the Sam Hill is this all about?"

"I'm not sure, but I'll get back to you." Josh pushed the end-call button and slipped his phone back in his jeans pocket.

The guard gave Jaycee another shove just as she reached the barn door. It was impossible to get a decent look at the interior even though there were overhead lights, but it appeared to be some kind of living quarters. The guard shut her inside the barn, slammed the door, engaged the slide lock and walked back to the house.

"Want to let me in on what's happening?" Grayson asked.

"I'm not sure. That agent down there is supposed to be on a leave of absence like me. How long before backup arrives?"

"Twenty minutes at least."

That was an eternity if those men were torturing Jaycee. And that was a strong possibility. The man hadn't exactly handled her with kid gloves when he'd maneuvered her into that barn. It was highly likely that her identity had been blown and that she was being held and forced to give information.

Which she wouldn't give easily.

Not Jaycee.

She wasn't just married to the badge, it was her soul mate. The only thing she actually cared about. She'd die—and get others killed—before giving up anything that would compromise an investigation. Even an unauthorized one.

He knew a lot about that, too, when it came to her.

Josh cursed under his breath. "Cover me. I'll move in for a closer look." And then he remembered that he wasn't talking to a fellow agent but rather his new boss. "I'll stay low and out of sight."

Grayson stared at him, his lips pressed together a moment, but then he nodded. "Call me if you spot trouble."

His phone was already on vibrate, and Josh drew his gun. That simple gesture gave him another jolt of flashbacks, but he wrestled the images aside and made his way back down the hill. It wasn't much of an elevation, but thankfully just enough to keep him hidden.

Grayson had left his truck parked on a ranch trail about a quarter of a mile away. That was no doubt where his brothers would park when they responded to the scene. They were all experienced cops and would know to do a quiet approach, but Josh wanted to finish his surveillance and be back in place with Grayson before they arrived. That way, they could discuss the best way to handle this.

Whatever *this* was.

He didn't see any guards on the side of the barn that wasn't facing the house, but he stayed low and used the vehicles for cover to make his way from the road and to the barn. No windows, of course. So he went to the back and spotted the door. It wasn't the type that'd normally be on a barn. More like a house door with a padlock on the outside.

But it wasn't locked now and was open just a fraction.

Still no sign of any guards, so Josh went closer and peered inside. It was dimly lit, the only illumination coming from an exposed bulb dangling in the center of the barn and a TV that'd been mounted high on a stall post. An old black-and-white movie flickered on the screen, but the sound was barely audible.

It took Josh a moment to pick through the darkness and shadows and spot Jaycee. She was sitting on an army-style cot, her elbows on her knees, her face buried in her hands.

She wasn't alone.

Josh saw two other women, both also on cots. One was reading a paperback and the other was staring up at the ceiling. What he couldn't tell was if there were any guards inside.

He didn't make a sound or move, but Jaycee's head snapped up, and as if she'd sensed he was there, her gaze zoomed straight toward him. Josh didn't need a lot of light to notice the relief in her eyes.

Quickly followed by something else.

Fear, maybe.

She shook her head, barely moving it, and she looked down, her loose shoulder-length hair sliding forward to conceal the sides of her face. She put her finger to her mouth in a stay-quiet gesture.

At least that was what Josh thought she was trying to do.

"What the hell's going on in there?" a voice boomed through the barn.

Josh glanced around and soon spotted the source. A large speaker mounted on one of the crossbeams. Next to it was a camera.

Hell.

Had they seen him?

Still no sign of either of the guards, but he got ready just in case he had to grab Jaycee and the others and run for cover.

"Nothing's wrong," Jaycee shouted. She stood, her back to Josh, and she put her hands on her hips. The sleeves of the bulky windbreaker billowed out like wings as she stared up at the camera. "What, I can't scratch my nose now without getting interrogated?"

The tone was the same old Jaycee. Smart mouth. In charge. But Josh could see that her hands were trembling.

"It looked like more than scratching your nose to me," the man on the intercom fired back. "You girls aren't trying to plan something, are you? Like another escape attempt? Because the last one didn't go so good, did it?"

So they were being held against their will. But why? And who was doing this?

"We learned our lesson about that already," Jaycee said, and the two others bobbed their heads in agreement.

The women were at the wrong angle to see Josh, and Jaycee made it even harder for them to spot him by stepping to the side. Positioning herself and that bat-wing windbreaker between the camera and him.

"So do I have permission to scratch my nose?" Jaycee yelled.

"Yeah. For now anyway. But if you try to break any more cameras, this time your roommates are gonna pay for it."

The moments crawled by, and there was a slight crackling sound. Jaycee's shoulders slumped, and she blew out a barely audible breath.

"I'm getting some air," she said to no one in particular, and she turned and headed toward the back door.

And Josh.

He saw it then. When she turned to the side and the windbreaker shifted. Her belly. Not flat as it'd been the last time they'd crossed paths.

Jaycee was pregnant.

Oh, man.

Josh forced himself to stay quiet and calm. And he also forced himself to think about the timing of all of this. It wasn't hard to remember the only time Jaycee and he had slept together. Because that was the same day he'd nearly died.

Five months ago.

Like the flashbacks, that hit him darn hard, like a heavyweight's fist to the gut. But he bit back any sound of surprise because if the guards heard him, it would likely get them killed.

Jaycee didn't look at him. In fact, she gave no indication whatsoever that she knew he was even there. She strolled to the back door, eased it open several inches farther than it already was and took a deep breath—like someone indeed getting a little fresh air.

"Don't move," she mouthed, her chin still lifted slightly in her fresh-air pose. "I broke the lens a couple of days ago with a rock, and they haven't gotten a replacement yet." She tipped her head to the tiny camera mounted on the eaves. "Right now, you're out of camera range for the one inside, and you need to stay that way."

He nodded, didn't move, except to drop his gaze to her stomach. "Whose baby is that?" he asked in a whisper.

She opened her mouth but then closed it just as quickly. Her attention sliced to the front door of the barn, and she whirled around to step in front of him.

Not a second too soon.

The door flew open, and Josh got just a glimpse of the armed goon as he rushed in.

And he pointed his rifle right at Jaycee.

Chapter Two

Jaycee cursed the panic that shot through her.

After months of being held captive, she should be used to having a gun pointed at her, but maybe that was something that never got *old*. Especially since each time one of the guards pointed a gun at her, they aimed at her stomach.

The one place that they knew would get her to cooperate.

She'd risk her own neck, but not the baby.

However, there was a new reason to do whatever they wanted so she could get the guard out of there. Josh's life depended on it, and sadly, so did hers and the other two women's, Marita and Blanca.

Her cell mates spoke only Spanish, but they understood enough English to know what they had to do. When the guard came in, they got to their feet, cowering. Both pregnant, like Jaycee, and both willing to do anything to protect the babies they carried.

"You sure you ladies aren't up to something?" the man growled.

Jaycee didn't know his name, but he was bald, ugly and big, which described every guard who'd been at the ranch over the past month.

This one came in at least several times a day, and he always made a repeat visit after bringing one of them back from the house. Maybe because he thought they were going to discuss whatever they'd seen or heard in there. Or maybe he thought they'd break some more cameras.

On each of these visits, Jaycee wished she could punch the guy in the face, take that rifle and get herself and the others out. But so far, escape had been impossible.

Maybe it still was.

She couldn't risk verbally warning Josh to stay put, but hopefully he would. He was a good agent. At least he had been before the shooting that'd nearly left him dead. If they survived the next few minutes, maybe she would be able to ask him how he'd found her and how he planned to get them all out.

And he'd better have a plan.

A darn good one.

Keeping herself directly in front of the door, Jaycee lifted the leg of her scrub pants to remind the jerk that since her attempted escape, she had been wearing an ankle monitor. One that would alert him if she did manage to get out of the barn. So far, she'd had no luck in getting the monitor off or disabling the Big Brother camera inside that watched them 24/7.

The jerk stared at them awhile longer. Jaycee didn't prolong his stay by glaring at him as she sometimes did. Her glare would rile him, she knew that for a fact, but a riled man just stayed longer.

She wanted him out of there *now*.

Finally, he mumbled something and got moving. So did Jaycee. She knew the angles of the camera and the blind spots. Well, one blind spot anyway. Even the bathroom that'd been added in the corner had no door. But she had learned that any time she moved into the remains of the horse stall just to the left of the back barn door that one of the jerks came running to make sure she was still there.

Definitely a blind spot.

"Stay low," she whispered to Josh, "and go in there."

Jaycee tipped her head to the stall. She had to get him out of the yard because the guard would soon be making a sweep of that area. Maybe he wouldn't come upon the backup that Josh had hopefully brought with him. If Josh had come alone, well, they were in trouble.

Without making a sound, Josh slipped through the bottom part of the door and into the stall.

"Keep your voice at a whisper," she warned him, angling her head away from the camera. She couldn't do that for long, either, or it would prompt another look-see from the guard. "There's a listening device on the post by the camera, but I've crammed bits of hay in it to muffle the sound."

She was sure he heard what she said, but his smoky blue eyes were planted firmly on her stomach.

Oh, *that*.

She owed him an answer to his question.

Since she'd first eyed that little plus sign on the home pregnancy test over four months ago, she'd wondered how she would spill this news. Josh wasn't exactly a family man. Thirty-four and had never even lived with a woman or been engaged. Jaycee didn't consider herself a relationship expert, but she figured that meant he hadn't planned on becoming a father this year.

And she didn't care.

This was *her* baby. She'd spent the last three and a half months protecting it, and she didn't intend to stop now. The only thing she needed from Josh was his help in getting them all the heck out of there.

Jaycee moved back to the door, propped her shoulder against the frame and pretended to examine the split ends on her hair. She spent a lot of time pretending to do mun-

dane things that concealed her eyes and mouth just so the
guards wouldn't be alerted that she was looking for a way
out of this Hades of a prison.

"Well?" Josh prompted.

Since an answer to that question would only waste time
and distract him, Jaycee went in a different direction. One
that would fully occupy his lawman's attention.

She hoped.

"There are four guards total," she explained. "At least
two are on watch at all times. And right now, there's a doctor inside. He's already given me and the two women here
checkups, but he'll examine the other four women who are
also being held captive in the house."

She risked a glance at Josh, and judging from the way
he looked at her—as if she'd lost her bloomin' mind—he
hadn't known those details.

"You did know about the captives, right?" she asked.
"And that this is a baby farm, and they're holding us
against our will?"

He shook his head.

That sucked the breath right out of her.

He didn't know. So why the devil was he here?

Josh shucked off his black Stetson and generally looked
as if he wanted to throw up in it. That only lasted a split
second, and he became the tough FBI agent again.

Or rather the hot cowboy cop.

That wasn't an FBI shield on his rawhide belt. It was
some kind of local badge. And he was wearing jeans and a
denim shirt that looked as if he'd been born to wear them.
Ditto for the rumpled chocolate-brown hair. Definitely not
FBI regulation length. Later, if she got the chance, she'd
tell him that it suited him.

Later, she'd tell him a lot of things.

And maybe he would listen.

Josh eased his phone from his pocket and fired off a text. "Will these men kill you if you try to escape?" he mouthed.

"Oh, yeah." She didn't have to think about that.

Jaycee had had enough experience with killers to know one when she saw one, and the guards were killers. She figured their boss was, too, though she'd yet to lay eyes on him. What she wanted to do was put a gun to his head and pull the trigger a couple of times. Harsh, yes, but he'd put a lot of women and babies through way too much misery.

"They've had me for three and a half months." She glanced at the other two women, who were pretending to do anything but look at her. "My Spanish sucks, but from what I've gathered, they were here about a month before I arrived."

"How'd this happen? How did they take you? *Why* did they take you?"

All good questions. Too bad her answers were somewhat lacking.

She moved to another section of her hair for the fake split-ends check. "I was coming out of a clinic after an OB visit. Another woman was walking out with me. Someone I didn't know. But she was close to her delivery date, and we were talking. Two men grabbed her. When I tried to help her, they hit us with Tasers."

Those memories were almost too painful to recall, but Jaycee had tried to brand every detail into her brain so she could catch the monsters once she was able to get free.

And she *would* catch them.

"I don't know what happened to the other woman," Jaycee continued. Again, a painful memory that clawed at her. She hadn't been able to save her, and now heaven knew what had happened to her and her baby.

"Why did they take you?" he repeated, his attention on her belly again.

"From what I've been able to find out, they kidnap women or force them into surrogacy and then sell the babies on the black market."

She let go of the hunk of her hair and moved on to nail-biting to cover the movement of her mouth. Except she was shaking enough that nail-biting didn't exactly seem like a pretense.

"They don't appear to know I'm an agent," Jaycee added.

And that was probably the only reason she was still alive.

This operation might not be huge, more like a sicko cottage industry, but it carried with it all sorts of felony charges. If the brains behind this thought she was FBI, they might not let her draw another breath.

And that would mean her baby wouldn't stand a chance.

Or maybe they knew she was an agent and were planning to use that in some way. Maybe to get information from her.

Josh's phone vibrated, and he glanced at the screen before answering it. "We're going to need a lot of backup," he whispered to the caller. "This is a black-market baby ring. At least four armed guards in the house. Four captives, too, and another three captives here in the barn."

Jaycee couldn't hear a word of what the caller said, and Josh's body-language clues shut down, too. No more emotion in his eyes.

Sometimes, like now, she got just a flash of the heat that'd once been between them.

Okay, more than a flash.

She got a full shot of the attraction that'd landed them in bed. Of course, with Josh's alarmingly handsome looks and long and lanky body, the attraction was a given. Even after all the bad that'd gone on between them.

He dropped his phone back in his shirt pocket and got into a crouching position. His gun ready. She hoped he had some kind of backup weapon that he could let her use.

"When I tell you and the women to get down, do it." Even though Josh whispered that order, it had some snarl to it. As if he'd considered that she might refuse. At this point, she wasn't refusing anything that would get her and all the captives out.

Jaycee managed a nod under the guise of more nail-biting, and since she didn't know what Josh's plan was, she stayed put. Waiting.

Praying, too.

"Is that baby mine?" he whispered.

She'd been expecting the question, of course, but Jaycee wasn't prepared for the suddenly clammy hands and her knees locking.

"Yes," she said.

She purposely didn't look at Josh because if he had another wave of nausea or some other unmanly response, he wouldn't want her to witness it. And besides, she didn't need the distraction of his response, either. Apparently, something was about to happen, something that would require her to shout to Marita and Blanca to get down before she did the same.

Something that would likely be dangerous.

Later, Josh and she could talk about the baby. Yelling would no doubt be part of that discussion, but for now, everything inside her screamed for her to do something—anything—to help with this escape.

And soon.

Jaycee felt useless standing there and waiting. Fortunately, she'd had a lot of practice with that during the past

months, and she'd learned some other things that Josh
needed to know.

"As far as I can tell," she whispered, "there are no working exterior cameras, and the computer inside the house
seems to be rigged just to monitor the camera here in the
barn and our ankle bracelets."

"How long will the doctor be here?" he asked. It was a
logical question, no hint of the baby bombshell she'd just
dropped on him.

"Maybe awhile. I think one of the women inside is in
labor."

That brought on some muttered profanity from Josh.
With good reason. It would be hard to escape with a woman
delivering a baby. As it was, it'd be difficult for some of
the women to run for cover. At least Marita, Blanca and
she weren't megapregnant, and they all appeared to be in
decent shape.

It seemed as if time practically came to a stop. Jaycee
couldn't say the same for her breathing. It was gusting
now, and there were beads of sweat on her face. The camera wouldn't pick up the sweat, but the breathing would
no doubt alert one of the bald goons.

As would her continued stay near the door.

Soon, very soon, one of them would show up to make
sure she wasn't up to no good and to order her back to
her cot.

Hoping to buy them some time from the guard check,
Jaycee partially closed the back door, leaving just a one-
inch gap—the way it usually stayed during the day. At
night, the guards locked them in with deadbolts. She went
back in the direction of the cot but didn't sit.

Best to stay on her feet, ready to react.

Marita and Blanca obviously picked up on her nonverbal
cues. Maybe the verbal ones, too, if they'd heard Josh and

her whispering. Blanca studied her from over the top of her paperback, and Marita kept volleying glances between Jaycee and the movie that she obviously wasn't watching.

Finally, Jaycee saw the movement in the gap in the back door. Not one of the guards. This was another cowboy with a badge. She got just a glimpse of him, but he had the same hair coloring and body build as Josh. A strong enough resemblance that this could be his brother.

The man peeked in, his gaze briefly connecting with Josh's, and Josh motioned for her to move to the door. She did, though Jaycee tried not to give anything away that the guards would detect.

"It's hot in here, huh?" she said to the others as a ploy to cover up why she was headed back in that direction.

She cracked opened the door again and saw that it was just the one lawman, *one,* and while he looked capable and in charge, that meant they were still outnumbered and outgunned.

As Josh had done, this guy dropped his gaze to her belly before he glanced in at the other women. Jaycee wasn't sure exactly what they wanted her to do, but she figured they had a minute at most before the guard would check to see why she'd reopened the door.

But she was wrong.

Not even a minute.

Just a couple of seconds.

The front door flew open, and the guard bolted inside. Not the one who'd come in earlier. This guy had a serious mean streak and had even slapped Blanca when she hadn't in his opinion moved fast enough.

"Hands in the air!" he yelled at the top of his lungs, and he shifted the gun not toward her but to the stall where Josh was hiding.

Jaycee braced herself for the guard to move closer so he could do a thorough search.

But that didn't happen.

The man pulled the trigger, and the shot blasted through the barn.

Chapter Three

The shot was deafening, and it roared through Josh's entire body. The flashbacks started again, but he shoved them aside. No time for that now.

"Get down!" he shouted to Jaycee, but she was already dropping to the floor. From the sound of it, so were the other two women.

He had no idea if they were out of harm's way because the *harm* just kept coming. The man fired another shot into the barn.

And then another.

Grayson threw open the back door just as Josh bellied out of the stall. Both of them fired at the shooter. Josh had no idea who'd taken down the man, but he fell, his rifle clattering to the ground.

"Let's move," Josh ordered the women.

Jaycee sprang up darn fast for someone who was pregnant, and she hurried to the other side of the barn to latch on to the two women. Josh stayed put, guarding the now-open front door where he was certain that it wouldn't be long before the other guards responded and came in firing.

"Mason and Dade are covering the house," Grayson let him know.

Mason and Dade were Grayson's brothers. Both were experienced deputies, but covering the house would be next to impossible with the gunmen inside. Unless there was some way to get the captives out so the guards couldn't use them as human shields.

Jaycee made it to the door, and Josh looked out, checking for those guards. By now they'd heard the shots, so why weren't they running to the barn in order for Mason and Dade to pick them off?

"Go ahead," Grayson insisted. "Get them out of here. I'll cover you."

Josh nodded, reached into his ankle holster to retrieve his backup weapon so he could give it to Jaycee. But it wasn't there, of course. He hadn't carried a backup since he'd left the FBI.

Big mistake.

But then, he'd never thought that he would run into something like this in the middle of nowhere.

With Grayson behind them and Josh in the lead, he maneuvered them out of the barn and to the corner away from the house. He glanced around first to make sure they weren't about to be ambushed. No one in sight. However, that didn't mean someone wasn't there, hiding.

"Don't use any of their vehicles," Jaycee warned. "I've seen the guards rig them with explosives."

Great. The guards had no doubt done that so the women couldn't use them to escape, but that was exactly what Josh had had in mind. One of those vehicles would have been the fastest way to get them out of there. Now they had to hoof it a good quarter to a half mile away.

And each step could be a fatal one.

He refused to think about the pregnancy now. Refused to think about anything that didn't involve survival.

"More backup's on the way," Grayson added.

They'd need it. Josh would have liked to have stayed with the women until they arrived because it was a risk to be outside like this. But staying put was just as much of a hazard as moving.

With his gaze firing all around, Josh led them to the front of the barn. No guards. But he spotted Mason and Dade on the hill where Grayson and he had been earlier. It was a good vantage point if anyone came out of the house, but no one appeared to be doing that.

The other two women were crying now, their breaths making hiccupping sounds with the sobs. Unlike Jaycee. She wasn't crying, and if Josh hadn't noticed her bleached-out color and jerky movements, he would have thought this was routine for her. But she also had one of her hands on her stomach.

Protecting her unborn child.

No, this wasn't routine.

She was scared spitless. And so was Josh—scared that he wouldn't get them safely out of there. He'd already faced death and made peace with it and his maker, but there'd be no peace if any of the women and their babies were hurt.

He glanced around at the position of the cars. There was a road and a heavily treed area on the backside of the hill.

"Have you ever seen guards in the surrounding woods?" Josh asked Jaycee.

"No. But sometimes replacement guards come in from the pasture on all-terrain vehicles. It's not time for the shift change, and I don't know where the replacement guards stay when they aren't here."

Later, that would need to be investigated, but they were a heck of a long way from the *later* point. For now, he just watched and made sure one of those ATVs didn't come barreling up on them from behind.

"Stay close and let's move," Josh ordered.

They ran the ten yards to the first vehicle so they could use it for cover.

But not for long.

If the kidnappers had indeed rigged it with explosives, then they might have a remote detonator. Josh hurried them to the next vehicle, a truck. And then the third, the only one left that would give them any protection if the gunmen in the house started firing.

"Move fast and don't look back," Josh told them, and he did exactly that.

Grayson would keep watch behind them. Dade and Mason would do the same to the right side. Josh would need to cover anything else, and that included those woods ahead.

Lots of places for gunmen to hide in there.

One of the women stumbled, but Jaycee latched on to her and kept her moving without missing a step.

He hated that he had to put them through this—a blasted footrace. This kind of stress couldn't be good for the pregnancies. But then the women had no doubt been through hell and back while in captivity. There was plenty of stress associated with that.

When they maneuvered away from the truck, Josh took a deep breath before he moved out into the open. He picked up the pace, jogging now, and they made it to the side of the hill.

Before he heard the shot.

It hadn't come at them. But it had come from inside the house.

Hell.

He prayed that none of the hostages had been hurt. His cousins must have feared the same thing because the shot sent Mason and Dade scrambling down the hill. They ran toward the same vehicles that Josh and the others had just used for cover. He knew the deputies couldn't wait any longer for backup. They had to move in and hope for the best.

"Go help them," Jaycee said to Grayson.

Josh met his cousin's gaze. It was a split-second glance, and he gave Grayson the nod. According to what Jaycee had told him, there were four women inside, and they were in grave danger. Mason and Dade would need all the help they could get.

Grayson tossed Josh his truck keys. "If you don't see me in ten minutes, go ahead and get them out of here and back to town. More backup should be here soon."

Josh didn't waste a second. It wasn't easy jogging with two sobbing pregnant women, but Jaycee helped. She pushed them from behind while she kept watch around him. When they made it to the road near the wooded area, Josh shifted positions, putting himself closer to the trees.

"If something goes wrong, get them in the ditch," he told Jaycee. Even though it was filled with several inches of water from the spring rains, it would still act like a bunker against flying bullets.

Each step seemed to take an eternity, but Josh finally spotted Grayson's truck ahead. He'd parked it just off the road, partially hidden beneath some towering oaks.

They had to run some more.

That put his heart higher in his throat, and the blasted wound on his chest started to throb again. But there was no way he'd give in to the pain and let it slow him down. Josh took one of the women by the arm and practically dragged her along those last yards.

Once he reached the truck, he used the keypad to unlock it, and even though it'd be a tight fit, he threw open the door and pushed them inside and onto the floor of the truck. The women stayed there, still sobbing, still praying in Spanish.

But Jaycee didn't stay down. She immediately threw

open the glove compartment and pulled out a Colt .45 and some extra ammunition.

"Was that man your brother?" she asked, tipping her head toward the house.

"Cousin. His brothers were on the hill."

She rolled down the window and got the Colt ready in case she had to fire. "Please tell me they all know what they're doing."

Josh did the same with his own weapon. "They do."

Grayson might have been sheriff of a small town, but Josh knew that he and his brothers had dealt with plenty of trouble over the past couple years.

Unfortunately, this was trouble of a different kind.

They waited, their attention pinned to the road ahead, their breaths bursting in and out. Josh hadn't checked the time when Grayson had given him that ten-minute rule, but he knew the minutes were ticking away.

"I don't want to leave them here," Josh said, more to himself than to Jaycee.

"Agreed. We have to get those other women out." Her gaze met his, and he saw her bottom lip tremble. "I think they kill the birth mothers once they're finished with them."

Oh, man. That did *not* help. Because there was no way he could drive back to safety when others were in danger.

Except Jaycee and these women were in danger, too.

And so were their babies.

Even though he didn't want his thoughts to go there, Josh couldn't stop them this time. "Why didn't you tell me about the baby?"

"I would have, but I didn't get the chance. I was kidnapped immediately after the doctor confirmed that I was pregnant." She had such a fierce grip on the Colt that her knuckles were turning white. "Are you going to ask me if the baby's really yours?"

"Don't have to." Josh looked away from her and put his attention back where it belonged—watching the area for any sign of one of those guards. "The baby's mine. You have a lot of faults, but lying's not one of them."

Any response she might have had to that was cut off when they saw Mason. He was flat-out running, and he was carrying a woman with a huge pregnant belly.

"I don't know her name," Jaycee said, "but I'm pretty sure she's the one in labor."

Josh looked for any signs of injury or blood. Didn't see any. Thank God. He jumped out of the truck and hurried over to his cousin.

"Take her," Mason growled and dumped her into Josh's arms. He turned as if to run back and help his brothers, but his phone vibrated, and cursing, Mason yanked it from his pocket.

Josh heard the footsteps behind him and reeled around as best he could, but it was only Jaycee.

"Here, I can help," she said, and she eased the moaning woman from Josh's arms to a standing position. Jaycee looped her arm around her waist and got her moving to the truck.

Josh was about to head there, too, but Mason's profanity stopped him. It wasn't unusual for Mason to curse. He wasn't a very friendly sort, but this bout of profanity was worse than his norm.

"The guards have one of the captives at gunpoint in the yard," Mason explained. "Get these women out of here now in case shots are fired."

"We can help," Jaycee repeated.

Mason shook his head, turned and delivered the rest

from over his shoulder. "One of the gunmen escaped out back. He could be headed your way."

There wasn't much color in Jaycee's face, but those words rid her of what little she had. She hurried, dragging the woman toward the truck.

"Go with them now, Josh!" Mason insisted.

That and the pregnant woman's sounds of pain spurred Josh to move. Jaycee maneuvered her into the truck, and the others helped pull her onto the seat.

"I can ride in the back," Jaycee said.

"You'll do no such thing," Josh argued. "Get inside and stay down."

She did. Well, she got in anyway. But she didn't stay down. Jaycee aimed the Colt at the bend of the road where Mason had darted out of sight. It was probably the route a gunman would take if he was coming after them.

Josh started the engine, threw the truck into Reverse and had just put his foot on the accelerator when he heard the sound. Not a shot from a rifle. Not this.

No.

It was much louder, and it literally shook the ground beneath them.

Something had exploded.

Chapter Four

Jaycee felt the vibration of the blast and saw the fear and concern jolt through Josh. It went through her, too, and she wanted to go back and try to save the others.

But that could be dangerous for the women Josh and the others had already managed to rescue.

Plus, the woman stretched out across Marita, Blanca and Jaycee's laps was clearly in labor. She was moaning and clutching her stomach. Jaycee had never been around anyone in labor, but she figured the woman was close to delivering.

Josh glanced at the woman, then at Jaycee. The worry and questions were still etched on his face, and she had to wonder what this was doing to him. Agents suffering from posttraumatic stress didn't usually have an easy time in a gunfight.

Or the shock of something totally unexpected—like fatherhood.

But Josh had gotten a double dose of both today. Hopefully, he'd be able to keep it together. She hoped the same for herself, too. She didn't have the nerves of steel that Josh had once accused her of having.

He'd accused her of a lot of things.

And sadly, most were accurate.

"Hang on," Jaycee told the woman in labor when she

made another of those loud moans. "You're safe, and we'll be at the hospital soon."

Jaycee hoped that was true on both counts. Josh was certainly driving as fast as he could, and both of them were keeping watch for those guards. So far, no one was following them.

Including any of Josh's cousins.

She prayed they hadn't been hurt, or worse, in the explosion.

"What's your name?" Jaycee asked the woman in labor. She'd need to give it to the doctor, but talking might also distract her from the pain. If that was possible.

"Grace Levitt," she answered through a sharp breath.

"All right, Grace, just hang in there a few minutes longer." Jaycee tried to sound calm. Failed miserably. But after everything she'd been through, she wondered if she would ever be calm again. Normal seemed way too far out of reach.

Jaycee put her hand on Grace's stomach so she could feel the contractions and time them. Yet something else the doctors would want to know. And Jaycee felt a contraction almost immediately.

Grace clamped her hand on Jaycee's shoulder. Her bruising grip was paired with more moans. Louder this time. And she lifted her hips. Jaycee didn't have to tell Josh to hurry. He no doubt knew they might have to deliver this baby in the cramped space.

The contraction finally subsided. Jaycee didn't have a watch, so she had to use the clock on the truck's dashboard to keep time. Barely two minutes had passed before Grace had another contraction.

Josh's phone buzzed, the sound shooting through the truck, and he managed to fish it from his pocket despite the fact that Marita was squished against him.

"Grayson," Josh answered, sandwiching the phone against his ear and shoulder. There was still no relief in Josh's expression, but thankfully at least one of his cousins was alive.

Jaycee couldn't hear what Grayson was saying. Couldn't tell if the news was good or bad. She could only wait and keep watch. They were getting close to the town of Silver Creek now, but that didn't mean the guards couldn't catch up with them and start shooting.

Josh finished talking with his cousin, but instead of telling her what was going on, he made another call.

"I'm calling the hospital," he said to her, and he told whoever was on the other end of the line that he was en route with four pregnant women who needed medical attention.

Jaycee opened her mouth to say that she was fine, but she didn't know that for sure. She'd been held captive for months, and even though she'd gotten plenty of checkups during that time, she couldn't trust any doctor working for black-market baby brokers.

Josh finally finished the call with the hospital, put his phone away and took the turn toward town. Just as Grace had another contraction.

"The house blew up," Josh relayed to her. "My cousins are okay. They weren't hurt in the explosion."

"But?" Jaycee asked because there was definitely a bad-news tone in his voice.

Josh didn't jump to answer, but his jaw muscles were stirring like crazy. "The guards escaped with the other three women."

Jaycee groaned. It was better than hearing they'd been killed, but it was still a major setback. "All the women who were staying in the house are close to delivering.

Once they have their babies, the guards will probably kill the women."

For once she was glad Blanca and Marita didn't understand a lot of English, though both women had no doubt figured out what was going on. They'd all seen the guards leave with babies, but never once had they seen one of the new mothers walk out of the ranch house.

Jaycee suspected they were being carted out in body bags at night.

"Grayson and the others are looking for them," Josh added.

Though it was the only thing they could do, it didn't seem nearly enough. The women were very pregnant and were no doubt being forced to run and do other things that their bodies and babies might not be able to handle. The guards wouldn't care a flying fig if the escape led to the women's deaths. They only cared about getting their hands on the babies so they could be sold like cattle.

"After we get Grace to the hospital," Jaycee murmured, "I want to help find them."

Josh made a sound. Definitely one of disapproval. "Going off half-cocked hasn't worked well for you or others in the past, has it?"

That stung. Because it was true.

Jaycee choked back her own moan. Barely. And just like that, the memories came.

All bad.

The old mixed with the new from her captivity. Five months ago, she'd been conducting her own investigation into some money laundering and hadn't been aware the operation already involved several undercover agents. Jaycee had only wanted to catch the piece-of-slime launderer who'd killed two women who happened to stumble upon his operation.

Instead, Jaycee had endangered the agents.

Josh had been shot and had nearly died during surgery. There'd been no *nearly* for his partner, Agent Ben Sayers. He'd been killed.

Someday she might learn how to live with that.

Might.

But for now it was just more bad memories added to the new ones from being held captive. She hadn't been beaten, but only because it could have caused her to miscarry. However, she'd certainly been slapped a few times and threatened daily. And yet the slaps and the threats hadn't been the worst of it. The worst thing had been not knowing what the abuse would do to her baby.

Grace moaned again, causing Jaycee's attention to snap back to the woman. Another contraction, and this one seemed even harder and longer than the others.

"We're almost there," Jaycee told her.

No lie this time. The town of Silver Creek was just ahead, and next to the sign for the city limits was one for the hospital. Josh went in that direction, and it was less than a minute before he pulled into the E.R. parking lot where there was a team of medics waiting for them.

The moment Josh stopped the truck, Jaycee hurried out. Blanca and Marita, too, so the medics could get to Grace.

"There's less than a minute between her contractions," Jaycee told them, and they got Grace on a gurney and whisked her away.

Jaycee was about to follow them when she found herself being placed on a gurney, too. The medics did the same to Blanca and Marita and wheeled them through the hospital doors. Josh was right there, hurrying along behind them.

"The doctor will be with you soon," a nurse said, and she put Jaycee into one of the E.R. cubicles. The nurse paused and looked at Josh. "Stay with her until I can get someone in here."

Josh nodded, though Jaycee was sure that staying with her was the last thing on earth he wanted to do. He no doubt wanted to check on his cousins or go after those escaped guards and missing women.

Anything that didn't involve having close contact with her.

She heard Grace's moans fading. Not because the woman had gotten quiet. But probably because she was being taken to Labor and Delivery and out of earshot. Jaycee hoped that she'd deliver a healthy baby and that she could soon put this nightmare behind her. Jaycee wished that for all the captives. Especially for those three who hadn't been rescued.

Soon, very soon, the quiet closed in around them, and because the room was small, Josh had no choice but to look at her.

Correction: he looked at her pregnant belly.

She saw the questions in his eyes. The doubts. Not about the baby's paternity. He was right about that—she wasn't a liar. Even though she had considered it. Briefly. After all, she was the last woman on earth who Josh would want carrying his child, and for a fleeting moment she'd wondered if he might want her to lie.

"I really did intend to tell you about the baby," she repeated, trying to answer some of those questions in his eyes. "I was worried that it'd cause you to blow a gasket or two, but I would have told you."

He nodded.

That was his only reaction. He certainly didn't deny that he would have been seriously upset to hear the news months ago. But then, Josh wasn't a liar, either.

"When's the baby due?" he finally asked.

"In four months."

Nine months after their weekend together in San Antonio. Their only weekend together. Yes, it'd been good.

Darn good.

But their last morning together, she'd seen that look in Josh's eyes and known he hadn't been looking for anything other than a short-term hookup. Old baggage, no doubt, since Josh had a love-'em-and-leave-'em reputation. So Jaycee hadn't given him an out and walked away.

Six hours later, he'd been shot.

And they'd learned about her rogue investigation that had collided with Josh's authorized one. If she had thought for one second that other agents were involved, she would have backed off. Of course, she hadn't asked a lot of questions when she'd gone after those money launderers and killers. Jaycee had only been thinking about justice.

Josh kept staring at her. Kept those questions in his eyes. She wasn't sure what he expected from her. Wasn't sure he'd tell her if he knew. But after all these months of being held captive, Jaycee had had time to figure out what she would say to him if she ever got the chance.

Well, now here was her chance.

"Look, I don't expect anything from you," Jaycee firmly stated. Giving him another out that he looked like he desperately needed. "I just wanted you to know because, well, because."

No reason to get into her old baggage. Or tell him that her own mother hadn't told her birth father that she was pregnant with Jaycee. Not until it'd been too late anyway. Jaycee had never had the chance to know her dad, and even though he was a less-than-stellar person, she'd sworn she would never do that to her child.

Even if the pregnancy was unplanned, like this one.

Josh's mouth tightened. His nostrils flared a bit. "It's my baby. Expect something."

That didn't sound like an offer of child support or shared custody.

It sounded like a threat.

And maybe it was.

Josh hated her. But she couldn't go back and undo this baby, and even if she could, she wouldn't. Though Josh might not believe her if she told him, she loved this baby with all her heart and would do anything to protect it.

"Expect something?" she repeated.

"Yeah," he snapped. And that was all he said for several moments. "Don't expect me just to walk away. I slept with you knowing there could be consequences, and I'm man enough to accept it."

She lifted her shoulder, ran her hand over her stomach. "But you probably didn't expect this consequence. We did use protection."

And clearly something had gone wrong. Jaycee had had a lot of time to think about every detail of that weekend, and while becoming pregnant had been the last thing on her mind, Josh was right. Sex, even safe sex, could make babies. And in this case, it had.

She waited to see if he intended to say more about consequences and expectations, but he didn't. He just kept staring at her and looking far better than he should have. His good looks weren't something he worked at. They were just there. And even now, she felt that little tug that she always felt when she looked at Josh.

Even when he was glaring at her.

"How are you?" she risked asking. Normally it was a polite, rote question, but this time, she truly wanted to know. And she figured he wouldn't want her to know.

"Fine," he snapped.

Translation: he was *not* going to talk about this. But she had five months of catching up to do.

She glanced at the badge clipped to his rawhide belt. "You left the FBI?"

"For a while." His jaw muscles went crazy again. "I'm on a leave of absence."

"Because you're recovering from the gunshot wounds," she finished for him.

He made a sound, a rumble deep in his throat. No doubt a back-off warning. But Jaycee didn't listen to that warning. "You're a deputy sheriff?"

He nodded.

Getting information from him was like pulling teeth. "Well, the job seems to suit you."

The clothes, too. She'd known about his cowboy roots but had usually seen him in a suit or his undercover outfits. Now he wore jeans, a black T-shirt and boots. He had his Stetson in his left hand as if he'd always carried it there.

"Something wrong?" he asked. Definitely not a friendly question. "You're looking at my clothes."

Actually, she'd been looking at the man in the clothes, but it was best to keep that to herself. "I want to thank you again. If you hadn't discovered where the baby farm was—"

"I didn't discover it." His words were clipped. Almost angry. But Jaycee got the feeling that this particular anger was aimed at himself and not at her. "I got lucky, that's all. But I didn't get lucky enough to save those other women that the guards took."

No. But maybe that'd be remedied soon if the sheriff could find something at the now-destroyed ranch. Yes, it was a long shot, but it was the only shot they had unless the woman in labor could give them some much-needed answers.

Before Jaycee had a chance to rile Josh further with more questions, a nurse came back in. According to her nametag, she was Lillian Renfrew. She took Jaycee's blood pressure and temperature—both were normal. That was a good start, and Jaycee hoped everything else proved to be normal.

"The doctor wants you to have an ultrasound," the nurse said, and she started to wheel Jaycee out of the cubicle. However, she stopped when Josh followed them. "You can wait outside."

"He's the baby's father," Jaycee volunteered when Josh didn't budge or say anything. "If he wants to come, I don't mind."

It was another risk, saying that out loud, but Josh kept the same expression that he'd had since they arrived at the hospital.

He was one angry, confused man.

"I want to see the ultrasound," he insisted, not like an argument but more a declaration of war.

Nurse Renfrew nodded and took them to a room in another hall. There was a tech waiting for them, a middle-aged woman with brunette hair, and she didn't waste any time hiking up Jaycee's scrub top all the way to her breasts. The scrub pants came down too, all the way to her panty line.

Even though Josh had seen her stark-naked, this seemed way more intimate.

"You don't expect anything from me?" Josh mumbled under his breath. And he repeated it, using that same "declaration of war" tone.

Oh, so that was what was still eating away at him. Jaycee tried to make eye contact with him, but the tech moved between them and squirted some cold goop all over Jaycee's stomach.

"I've heard you say plenty of times that you weren't looking for marriage or a family," Jaycee reminded him.

The tech finally went back to the other side of the gurney. Josh's and Jaycee's gazes met.

Collided, actually.

"I wasn't looking to be a father," he stated, enunciating each word as if she were mentally deficient, "but I'm not running from it, either. That's my baby, and he or she should expect everything from me. Because he or she will get just that—*everything*."

He stopped, muttered some profanity. Rubbed his forehead. And got his teeth unclenched. "I'm glad you made it out of there." His voice was a lot softer than before.

"Yes. Thank you for saving me."

He nodded, and she hoped that meant they'd reached a tentative truce. No time to linger on it, though, because the tech started moving the wand over Jaycee's stomach. She immediately saw something.

Maybe the heart beating.

The images weren't very clear so Jaycee didn't know exactly what she was looking at, but it was her baby. And she hadn't expected that seeing all those blurry images would pack such a wallop.

"Is the baby okay?" Josh asked.

Jaycee was glad he had said that because her mouth was suddenly bone-dry, and her heart was pounding. She was terrified that this ordeal had been too much for her precious child.

"Everything appears to be okay. Good, solid heartbeat. Good movement." The tech stopped, volleyed glances at both of them, her attention finally stopping on Jaycee. "How much did your doctor tell you about the pregnancy?"

Oh, God. Just like that the fear returned. "Is something

wrong? I had other ultrasounds, but they kept the screen hidden from me. Did they do that because something's wrong with the baby?"

The woman shook her head. "I don't think anything's wrong." She glanced at the screen again. "But the doctor will need to see the images and talk to you." She paused, cleared her throat. "Some people just don't want to know the sex of the baby, and sometimes we can't tell. This time, we can."

The relief came as fast as the fear. Nothing was wrong.

"Do you want to know the sex of the baby?" the woman asked.

"No," Jaycee said at the same moment that Josh said, "Yes."

"I've just had too many surprises today," Jaycee added. "I'd like to hear it at a time when I'm not about ready to jump out of my skin. But you can tell him," she said to the tech. "I'll just cover my ears."

Jaycee did. Closed her eyes, too. And when she opened them, she couldn't detect a darn thing from Josh's expression.

"I'll show the ultrasound to the doctor," the tech said, turning off the machine. "Someone will be in shortly to take you back to the E.R."

The tech had hardly made it out the door when Josh's phone buzzed. Just like that Jaycee was reminded of the three missing women and the nightmare that wouldn't end until they were all safe.

Josh looked at the phone screen. "It's Grayson," he told her. And he clicked the speaker function.

"How are the women?" Grayson asked.

"One's in labor. The other three are being checked out now."

"Good. Stay there with them, and if they're feeling up

to it, get statements from them. I'm trying to get a CSI team out here ASAP."

Josh shook his head. "What's going on?"

"I'm not sure." Grayson paused a heartbeat. "But we found something."

Chapter Five

Something.

Yeah, it was that all right. Josh looked at the items that had been collected from the rubble of the house that had exploded.

A laptop.

Or rather, what was left of it.

Josh wasn't sure they could recover anything from it, but there was a tech from the crime lab already working on it.

There were also bits and pieces of paper. Several coffee mugs that would be processed for prints. Some shoes.

And a badge in its black leather case.

It was pretty beat up, as if someone had used it for a mini punching bag, but Josh had no trouble recognizing it as one issued to FBI agents.

Beside him, Jaycee pulled in her breath when she saw it. "Is the badge mine?"

Grayson nodded. "There's enough of the identification card for us to confirm it's yours."

"Oh, God," she murmured and sank down into the chair next to the desk. "I didn't have it on me when they took me. That means they got it from my apartment."

And more than that, it meant they knew who she was.

She looked up at Josh as if she expected him to have

some answers, but he didn't. The only thing that he was certain of was they would have indeed killed Jaycee once the baby was born. No way would they let an agent go free.

"But why steal my badge?" she asked, volleying glances at both Grayson and him.

"We're not sure." Grayson motioned to the laptop. "But we're hoping the info's recoverable. Plus, we've contacted your supervisor, Philip McCoy, to let him know what's going on, since he thought you were on a leave of absence this whole time."

"I did let him know I was taking some time off," Jaycee said. "I was trying to deal with what happened so I told him I wasn't sure when I'd be back to work—if ever," she added in a mumble.

"That's why he didn't push to find you," Grayson continued. "Now that he knows what happened, he'll check to make sure no one used your badge to get into the FBI building."

Where the person would have had access to all sorts of files and people. Of course, the San Antonio office where Jaycee was assigned wasn't that large, so someone would have noticed a stranger trying to use Jaycee's badge to gain entrance. If that had happened, it would have been a red flag for McCoy that something was wrong.

Grayson opened his mouth to add more, but his phone rang. It was the third call that had come through since Josh arrived with Jaycee ten minutes earlier.

Josh looked down at her. At her exhausted face. Her shoulders were slumped. There were dark circles under her eyes. She was biting her bottom lip. Every part of her body language told him she was tired and worried. Heaven knew what all this stress was also doing to the baby.

"I'll get you out of here soon," he let her know.

But that was another problem.

He'd learned on the drive over that Jaycee no longer had an apartment. Since she hadn't paid her rent, her things had been moved to storage and the place had been rented out to someone else. She had no family to speak of. And he wasn't sure how she would feel about going to a hotel with the armed guards still at large, especially since those guards knew her identity.

Heck, Josh wasn't sure how he felt about it. After all, if Jaycee was in danger, so was the baby.

His baby.

Those two words kept running through his head. It'd been just words until he saw the ultrasound, and then it had felt like an avalanche. For a few seconds. And then he'd felt a whole lot more. The love for a baby he hadn't even known he wanted until today.

The wound on his chest started to throb. A bad reminder of his past with Jaycee. He was a long way from forgiving her, but he wouldn't let the past stand in the way of giving their baby the best protection he could.

Grayson finished his call, and for the first time in hours, he looked a little relieved. "That was the hospital. The woman in labor just gave birth to a healthy baby girl. The other two women are fine, too. We're working on getting them all back with their families."

"Good," Jaycee said under her breath, and she repeated it. "But what about the three women and the guards? Any sign of them?"

"Nothing." The frustration returned to Grayson's expression. "But I need you to think. Did you see or hear anything that would give us a clue as to where they would have taken the women?"

"No." And she didn't hesitate, either. "Any time I would go in the house for a checkup, I'd try to look around. Try to figure out who these men were. I don't remember hearing or seeing anything. I'm so sorry," Jaycee added, and her voice cracked.

There was no telling how many nightmarish memories she had of her time as a captive. It sickened Josh to think of all those women and babies being in constant danger for months on end.

Grayson glanced at Jaycee's pregnant belly. Then at Josh. "I gather that you two were once…involved?"

Josh nodded. "The baby's mine."

"You think maybe that's why Jaycee was taken? Maybe so someone would have leverage over you? The baby of two FBI agents is plenty of leverage."

Yeah. It was.

Jaycee made a sound of agreement, too. "But if I was their initial target, they covered it well. I was kidnapped with another woman, and it certainly seemed as if they wanted just her. They only took me because I tried to fight back."

That didn't help the throbbing pain in Josh's chest, either. Of course, he couldn't have expected Jaycee to stand there and do nothing. He wouldn't have.

Grayson released a long, weary breath. "I can get Jaycee's statement tomorrow. Why don't you go ahead and take her to the ranch so she can get some rest?"

Jaycee's eyes widened. "The ranch? With your family?" She shook her head. "That's probably not a good idea."

"I have five brothers," Grayson explained to her. "All in law enforcement. The ranch is safe, or at least it is for now. My dad's a widower, and he's getting married this weekend. There'll be a lot of people in and out for the arrangements and for the ceremony itself. We'll need to add some security when that starts happening."

Grayson didn't mention those armed guards coming back for her, but they all knew it was a strong possibility.

Jaycee was a dangerous loose end, and whoever was running the black-market operation wouldn't want her around to give the cops any details about her captivity.

"Come on," Josh insisted, and he was thankful she didn't argue.

He did a thorough check of the parking lot and the street before he led her outside and to his truck. Josh didn't see anything suspicious, but he hurried anyway and got them on the road toward the ranch.

"I need to remember something," Jaycee murmured. "Anything that'll help us find those women."

Since she'd been held for nearly four months, there were a lot of memories and details to sort through. "Did you ever see the laptop that was recovered from the rubble?"

She stayed quiet a few moments. "Yes, on the kitchen table about two weeks ago. I can't be sure it was the same one, but I remember seeing one there."

Maybe that meant the laptop had been at the house long enough for it to contain something to blow this case wide open.

"What about the checkups you had?" he asked. "Did the same person do them each time?"

"Yes. Caucasian male, about six feet tall, 170 pounds, light brown hair. He always wore a surgical mask, but if he hasn't altered his hair, I think I could pick him out of a photo lineup."

It'd be a bear to sort through all the doctors in the state, but Josh made a mental note to ask the analysts at Quantico to work on it. They might get lucky.

"You know if the baby's a boy or girl," she said.

The out-of-the-blue comment threw him for a moment. But Josh just nodded. "Why? You want to know?"

She shook her head. Groaned softly. "This seems crazy, huh? Me pregnant with your baby."

Yeah, it did. Of course, when they'd made the baby, it was before the shooting, when they were still on good terms. They weren't on good terms now, but like the flashbacks he'd been having, Josh was going to have to put that aside, too.

"I'm scared of you," Jaycee went on. "Scared you'll try to fight me for custody or something."

Again, the comment threw him, and he wasn't sure it was a good thing to have that possibility out in the open like this. Especially since he had plenty of other things to work out in his head.

"I want to be part of the baby's life," he settled for saying. It was a safe response. And an honest one. He might want more than just a *part*, and while he didn't say that aloud, it seemed as if Jaycee picked up on it.

She swallowed hard. "And that's what scares me. You have a normal life. Good roots and a law-abiding family. I don't have any of that."

She didn't. Both her parents had served hard time for an assortment of crimes, and he'd heard that Jaycee had been brought up in foster care. His parents had divorced when he was a kid, and his mother had left, but it wasn't the same. So yeah, by her standards he did have a normal life.

Well, except he was suffering from PTSD and might never recover. That wouldn't look good on a custody challenge if that was what he decided to do.

He took the final turn to the ranch, and Jaycee got an immediate glimpse of his "normal" life. There were now six houses on the grounds, assorted barns, outbuildings and miles and miles of pasture for the horses and cattle raised on the ranch.

"Five of my cousins had houses built after they got married and started families of their own," he explained.

"My other cousin, Mason, lives in the main house with his wife and dad."

"The one who's getting married this weekend."

"That's right. Boone Ryland. He's marrying a former deputy, Melissa Garza. She retired recently, and that's how I got the job."

Jaycee made an idle *uh-huh* sound, but her attention wasn't on anything he'd pointed out, but rather the children in the fenced playground on the side of the main house.

"There's so many of them," she whispered. "It looks like a day care."

It did. "They're all kin. Last count, my cousins have nine offspring, and Mason and his wife have one on the way."

And at the moment it seemed that all nine were out playing while a few of their moms watched.

Josh slowed when he reached the playground. The moms all waved. One of the kids, Kimmie, who was four years old, saw him and blew him a kiss.

"The little red-haired girl seems to like you," Jaycee mumbled.

She did. Though Josh couldn't understand why. He'd never been comfortable around kids, and they seemed to be uncomfortable around him. All except for Kimmie. That gave him a little hope that his own child might feel the same way.

He drove past the playground to the back part of the east pasture to a weathered-looking barn and pulled to a stop in front of it.

"You live *here?*" Jaycee asked, sounding skeptical and surprised.

Another dose of his version of normal. "The top floor's been converted into an apartment. But if you like, I can get you a guest room in the main house."

She glanced back in the direction of the children and their moms. Then the barn. "Your place will be fine."

Josh bit back a smile. Barely. That'd been his reaction when he'd first returned home. "The kids grow on you," he confessed.

At least that's what he'd heard anyway.

He led her up the side stairs to the studio-style apartment. Even though the barn was isolated, it still had all the conveniences of a real house.

Jaycee paused in the doorway, her gaze moving over the room. But there wasn't much to see. Other than the bathroom, it was just one big open space, with the modest kitchen and sitting area on one side and his bed on the other. There were clothes scattered on the floor. Dishes in the sink. Just the way he'd left it when he'd gone to work earlier.

"You haven't been sleeping well," she commented. Jaycee tipped her head to the unmade bed. The covers were in a tangled heap. His prescription pain meds were on the nightstand.

"Sometimes," Josh settled for saying.

He went in, too, shutting the door behind them, and he tossed his keys onto the kitchen counter before he set the security alarm. A first for him since the ranch had always felt so safe, but nothing felt safe enough now.

"A security system in a barn?" she murmured.

"Yeah. Mason had it installed a few years ago after some intruders managed to get onto the grounds. Most of the buildings have security."

That put some renewed fear on her face.

"It's all right," he assured her. "It was nothing recent. Nothing to be concerned about."

But of course, they were both still concerned.

Jaycee inched across the room to the huge bay window

at the far end of the room. It was late afternoon, and the butter-colored sun hit her just right to spotlight her.

Josh felt that punch of heat.

A punch he definitely didn't want to feel but, like the other things going on in his head today, he couldn't seem to push this one aside.

"Should we try to clear the air?" Jaycee asked with her back to him.

"No." And he didn't have to think about it. No way did he want to discuss the shooting with her. Besides, they were well past the air-clearing stage.

She turned, met his gaze. "Then at least let me say I'm sorry."

He didn't want to hear it, but it would have been petty to blast her for an apology that he couldn't accept. Josh was still trying to figure out what to say when she crinkled her nose and slid her hand over her belly.

"Are you okay?" he quickly asked.

"It's just the baby kicking."

It didn't seem to be a painful experience, and she certainly didn't ask Josh to share it. Instead, she went to the bed and started fixing the covers.

"I think I'll take a nap, if you don't mind," she said.

"Don't mind at all." And he went to the bed to help her straighten the sheets. To say this was an awkward moment was a huge understatement. Beds and Jaycee were never a good idea, even when it was the only option they had.

Thankfully, he had an immediate distraction. His phone made a soft dinging sound to indicate he had a text. Josh pulled it from his pocket and saw Grayson's name on the screen.

This probably wasn't good news. And it wasn't short and sweet, either. It had an attachment. Grayson started by saying the reason he didn't call was because he hadn't wanted to wake Jaycee in case she was sleeping.

But there was a lot more than that in the message.

"You know the name Bryson Hillard?" Josh asked, reading through it.

Jaycee repeated the name, shook her head. "Never heard of him. Why?"

"The tech found his name on the laptop they recovered from the house."

Another headshake. "Who is he?"

"A wealthy San Antonio businessman. No criminal record. Grayson plans to bring him in for questioning first thing in the morning."

"I want to be there," she insisted.

Josh didn't try to talk her out of it. Heck, he wanted to be there, too. Because this was personal now. The idiot responsible had put his unborn child and countless others in danger, and if this Bryson Hillard had anything to do with it, Josh wanted to know. And *confront* him.

He scrolled through the rest of the email, and the reading came to a jarring halt when he saw the last sentence.

Hell.

He repeated the mental profanity when he opened the attachment.

"Once I take a nap," Jaycee said, obviously not noticing his change of expression, "I'll make some calls and find another place to stay."

Josh finished reading the message before he went to the window and closed the blinds.

When he turned around, Jaycee was waiting, her mouth slightly open, and she had a white-knuckle grip on the bed post. "What's wrong? What happened?"

Josh debated how much he should tell her and decided she had to know the truth. "You can't leave," Josh told her.

"You'll have to stay here for the night, because those missing guards are looking for you. They left you a message nailed to the door of your old apartment."

He walked closer and held up his phone for her to see the message that one of the deputies had photographed.

Jaycee's gaze darted over the words, and she pressed her trembling fingers to her mouth. "Oh, God."

Chapter Six

The images kept coming at Jaycee in the nightmare. Images of the explosion. Of their escape and the armed guards.

Especially of the women who hadn't been lucky enough to get away.

When she could take no more of those brutal images, Jaycee forced herself to wake up, and she jackknifed to a sitting position.

And nearly smacked right into Josh.

He wasn't in the sleeping bag on the floor, which was the last place she'd seen him before she dozed off. He was there right next to the bed, leaning over her. His hands were lifted as if he were about to give her a hug. But the look in his eyes was pure concern.

"I was about to wake you," he said. "You were having a bad dream."

Yes, and it'd been a doozy, no doubt spurred on by the message the guards had nailed to the apartment door. Just two little sentences, but it was the stuff of nightmares and a serious guilt trip.

Agent Finney, you sealed those women's fates when you escaped. Thanks to you, they'll all soon be dead.

It shouldn't have surprised her that the kidnappers had addressed her as Agent Finney. She'd already learned that they knew who she was. It was the other part of the message that had caused the tightness in her chest. And the nightmares.

Thanks to you, they'll all soon be dead.

She had no doubt that these men would kill in retaliation, but she prayed they wouldn't harm the women until they'd delivered their babies. That would give Josh and her some time to find and rescue them.

"Any sign of the men or the hostages?" she asked, and Jaycee held her breath, waiting for Josh's answer. She didn't dare ask if any bodies had been found, because she wasn't sure she could take the answer.

"None." Josh put down his hands but didn't move off the bed. He stayed right there, looming over her.

And he was naked.

Jaycee did a double take.

Okay, not naked. Just shirtless.

She had a good view of not just those toned abs and pecs but also the scar. It was several inches long and slashed across his otherwise perfect body. Even though it was well healed, she figured the ashy white line would never go away.

The memory of it certainly wouldn't.

"Sorry," he mumbled, following her gaze. "I was changing when I heard you call out my name."

She had? Jaycee didn't remember saying his name, but Josh had certainly been in the nightmare. This time, instead of getting her and the three other women to the truck, he'd been lying in a pool of blood.

Yes, definitely a nightmare.

She didn't want to be the reason that he took another bullet, but it had come too close to happening yesterday.

Too bad she couldn't distance him from all of this, but she knew what his response would be if she even tried.

No way.

And she couldn't blame him. If their situations had been reversed, she would have wanted to keep him close, too. To protect him from those note-leaving guards who seemed to enjoy tormenting them.

"You're sure you're okay?" he asked, examining her eyes, then her face.

His attention dropped lower, and that was when she realized the bulky T-shirt that he'd lent her had fallen off her shoulder to expose a lot of her left breast. And there was a lot more to her breasts these days, since the pregnancy had made them fuller.

Jaycee quickly fixed the shirt situation, and it was her turn to mumble that she was sorry. Not that Josh would have found her attractive anyway, what with her pregnant belly just beneath those fuller breasts.

But she immediately rethought that.

There was indeed some heat in his cool blue eyes. Of course, there'd always been heat between them. That wasn't their problem. Their problem was the scar on his chest, and since she was responsible for that, it would always stand between them.

"Yeah," he muttered as if he knew exactly what she was thinking. And he got up, went to the kitchen area and poured himself some coffee.

"Does it still hurt?" Jaycee asked. "The scar," she clarified when he gave her a puzzled look.

"Sometimes. There was some muscle damage." And with that tiny bit of info, he turned away. Everything in his body language indicated that the subject was off-limits.

Jaycee huffed, looked at the alarm clock on the night-stand. It was 7:00 a.m.

Good grief. Where had the time gone?

She'd fallen asleep shortly after eight, which meant she'd really racked up some serious snoozing time. Of course, this was the first morning in months that she hadn't woken up as a captive.

Well, a real captive.

She certainly wasn't a free woman, not as long as those men were at large. She'd essentially have to stay in hiding until they were caught. Or do something to catch them herself. Jaycee was leaning toward the latter, but she wasn't sure how to go about that.

"I talked to your supervisor a little while ago," Josh went on. "He officially put you on a leave of absence so we'd have time to sort this out. The FBI will assist with the investigation any way they can."

"That's good." After the danger was over, she'd have a job waiting for her. One less thing to worry about.

"Grayson's wife brought over some clothes and toiletries earlier," Josh said, tipping his head to a small suitcase next to the door.

Jaycee hadn't heard their visitor or Josh up and moving around, and that unnerved her. She had to be more vigilant. Had to do more to keep herself safe.

Starting with finding another place to stay.

She'd need to make some calls once she had washed up and changed. And Jaycee didn't want to think about how Josh would react to her decision. Of course, he might be a little relieved. Having her under the same roof couldn't be any easier for him than it was for her.

She got up, took the suitcase with the clothes and headed to the bathroom to shower and change into a loose yellow cotton maternity dress. In fact, all the clothes were maternity, but that shouldn't have surprised her, either. Not with all the children she'd seen running around the ranch.

Josh was on the house phone when she came out of the bathroom. He quickly ended the call, but he'd no sooner done that when his cell rang. The sound shot through the room and caused her to gasp.

Get a grip.

She wasn't the gasping type, and what she needed to settle her nerves was her gun and her badge. A little bit of normalcy might go a long way toward helping her get through the rest of this day.

"It's Grayson," Josh said, and he hit the speaker function on his phone. "Please tell me you have good news," he said to his cousin.

"Some. Two of the women, Marita and Blanca, will be headed back home today. They're sisters, and they said their family is very poor, and their father basically sold them to a man who said he wanted them to work as maids. Instead, he took them to the baby farm where they were inseminated."

Josh's grip tightened on his coffee cup. His mouth tightened, too. "Do the women know the fathers of their babies?"

"No. But they agreed to have an amniocentesis. That's a procedure to test the amniotic fluid, and it'll give us the DNA of the father. Or fathers, whatever the case might be. If he's in the system, we could get a match."

It was another long shot, but better than nothing. Besides, someone who would force women into surrogacy probably did have a police record.

"The other woman will be able to leave the hospital tomorrow," Grayson went on. "Her ex fathered her child, so no need to do DNA tests. She was hiding from the guy. Had a restraining order on him, but he kept finding her and assaulting her. So she moved to San Antonio and was living under an alias when she was kidnapped and taken to the baby farm."

"She won't be going back to the ex, will she?" Jaycee asked.

"No. We're relocating her to a different city."

Good. If she'd been through anything like Jaycee had, then being rescued shouldn't take her from the frying pan and into the fire.

"So she and the baby are okay?" Josh asked.

"Fine. The woman didn't have a scratch on her."

Somewhat of a miracle considering their escape, and it was a dose of good news that Jaycee needed. However, she could hear a "bad news" hesitation in Grayson's voice.

"Did the men leave me another message?" she came out and asked.

"Not that we've found." He paused. "But we did find something else. The tech was able to recover some of the data on the laptop's hard drive. A lot more than just Bryson Hillard's name. It appears there are more baby farms. Maybe dozens of them scattered throughout the state."

Oh, mercy.

It sickened her to think of all those women and their babies in danger.

"According to some emails on the hard drive," Grayson continued, "the people behind this kidnapped pregnant women who wouldn't be immediately missed. Homeless women, runaway teens or those without families."

Like her.

Judging from what Jaycee had found out the night before, her supervisor had simply thought that she'd gone off the deep end because of Josh's shooting and had taken a long leave of absence. She had gone off the deep end. But that hadn't been the reason for her disappearance.

"How many women are we talking about?" Josh asked.

"Dozens at least. Not all came from Texas. Some were illegal immigrants or those on the run from the law, and some appear to have been forced into becoming surrogates like Marita and Blanca."

Josh muttered some profanity. "And there were no missing persons reports filed on any of these women?"

"A few, but not enough for any law enforcement agency to connect the dots."

Jaycee huffed, but she knew that unless there was a pattern, the FBI wouldn't have picked up on it. "What about the people paying for the babies? Any info about them on the hard drive?"

Grayson made a sound of frustration. "They're all listed by case numbers with no personal details. We can try to match the numbers with adoptions filed during that time, but I'm betting the people who paid for these babies didn't file papers."

Jaycee was betting the same thing. She took a deep breath before she asked the next question. "Were the birth mothers murdered?"

"Don't know yet. We don't have identities on the women. Well, with the exception of you and the ones who were rescued yesterday."

She immediately thought of something. "What about the woman who was kidnapped the same time as me? She was at the Hawthorne Medical Center in San Antonio, so there should be a record of her name on the appointment schedule."

"I'll check and see what I can find," Grayson assured her. "But since these people stole your badge, it's possible you were their primary target all along."

That sent a chill right through her. Heaven knows what these monsters had planned to do with her baby. And with her. But she figured they hadn't had anything good in mind. Maybe they'd wanted to use the baby to force her into doing something illegal.

Maybe Josh, too.

Her baby could have become the ultimate bargaining tool, since there were a lot of things that two FBI agents could cover up or overlook in criminal investigations.

"We'll keep digging," Grayson added, and he ended the call.

Jaycee didn't even try to hide her frustration. "That wasn't the way I'd wanted to start the morning," she mumbled.

"No," Josh quietly agreed. "But at least we have a possible lead. If we get a DNA match from Blanca's and Marita's babies, then we can interrogate the birth father. Or fathers. They could help us find the person who honchoed this mess."

Yes, it was a good lead, but it didn't seem nearly enough considering all the lives that were at stake.

"Coffee?" he asked, raising his cup.

Jaycee shook her head because the smell made her a little queasy. "But I wouldn't say no to some toast or milk. Or a doughnut." She wasn't hungry, but she should eat something for the sake of the baby.

His left eyebrow lifted. "A doughnut?"

"Yeah, I've been craving them in between the bouts of morning sickness."

But her suddenly jittery stomach wasn't a result of morning sickness. Probably more nerves than anything else. After all, Grayson had just told them some disturbing things.

Plus there was Josh.

Yet something else disturbing in a totally different way. She was in a very confined space with a shirtless man whom she'd always found attractive. His jeans didn't help, either.

They were snug in all the right places.

And despite the fact that she was five months' pregnant and coming down from a horrible ordeal, she felt the heat trickle through her.

Their gazes met.

Held.

And Josh gave a heavy sigh before he turned around and put two pieces of bread in the toaster. He also crossed the room, grabbed a shirt from the closet and put it on. It still didn't help. Jaycee had a much too vivid memory of how he looked without it.

"Sorry, no doughnuts," he said. "If it'd make you more comfortable, I repeat my offer—you can move to one of the guest rooms in the main house."

"With all those people? No thanks. I can call some friends." If she still had any, that is.

Josh stared at her. "FBI friends?"

Jaycee shrugged. Actually, she didn't have a lot of friends in the FBI because she often worked alone and undercover for long stretches. That didn't give her a lot of socializing time. Ironically, before the shooting, Josh had been her closest friend, and she doubted he'd now classify her as such.

"Look, you've already done so much," she said, "and I don't want to keep imposing on you."

"It's not an imposition." His gaze dropped to her stomach. "And I'd rather be the one protecting you."

A burst of air left her mouth. Not quite a laugh. "I'm a trained agent just like you. The kidnappers took my gun, but if you give me another one, I'll be pretty good at protecting myself."

Oh, no. He got that mule-headed look. The one that let her know he wasn't going to back down on this.

"You're a *pregnant* trained agent." Even though the toast popped up, Josh ignored it and walked closer to her. "I know this isn't what you want to hear, but that baby changes everything."

Jaycee wanted to be mule headed, too. Mercy, did she want that. But he was right. The pregnancy did change things. She'd fought her way out of plenty of bad situations, but fighting wasn't much of an option now because it'd put the baby at risk.

"No one will protect you like I will," Josh added, and he jammed his thumb against his chest.

The moment seemed to freeze, and she thought he was about to move toward her. To pull her into his arms. Jaycee wasn't stupid and knew it wouldn't be for a steamy kiss that her body seemed to want.

Bad.

But Josh looked to be on the verge of giving her something else she needed. A good old-fashioned hug.

It didn't happen, though, because his phone rang again, and the moment was gone. He drew in a hard breath and stabbed the button to put the call on speaker.

"Josh," she heard Grayson say. "I think Jaycee and you should get down here to the sheriff's office right away. Our suspect, Bryson Hillard, just walked in. He's got a lawyer with him, and he says he'll talk if he can speak to one of the former hostages."

In other words, *her.*

Jaycee pulled her breath. Waited.

It didn't take long for Grayson to continue. "Bryson says he knows who's running the baby farms."

Chapter Seven

"You recognize either of them?" Grayson asked Josh and Jaycee.

Josh looked through the one-way mirror and into the interview room of the Silver Creek sheriff's office where Bryson Hillard and his attorney, Valerie DeSilva, were seated. Both appeared to be in their mid-forties. Both wore nondescript business clothes. Bryson had salt-and-pepper hair, conservative but expensively cut. Nothing much conservative about Valerie's hair. It was flame red, short and choppy—the style of a much younger woman.

"Never seen them before," Josh answered.

Jaycee shook her head and echoed the same, her attention returning to the background report on the two that Grayson had given them when they'd first arrived at the sheriff's office. They were all anxious to hear whatever information Bryson had, but Josh knew that Grayson needed to be armed with info so he could convince the man to talk without Jaycee's help.

Just in case this was some kind of ruse to get to her.

Josh certainly couldn't rule it out, especially since the guards knew who she was and also knew that she was in protective custody in Silver Creek. They'd left that threatening note, and if they'd been that brassy, Josh figured they wouldn't hesitate to send someone right into the sheriff's office so they could launch another kidnapping attempt.

There was just one problem with that theory.

Neither Bryson nor Valerie looked capable of kidnapping unless they had help, and lots of it. Of course, those three missing guards would be plenty of help, and if he was looking at the faces of the people in charge of the baby farms, Bryson and Valerie could have those guards waiting nearby.

Josh was in such deep thought and way too much on edge that he nearly reached for his gun when he spotted the movement out of the corner of his eye. But it wasn't a threat. It was one of the other deputies. She had a cup of coffee in one hand and was balancing a large box of doughnuts in the other.

"I'm Bree," she said to Jaycee, and she slid the doughnut box on the table. "Married to Grayson's youngest brother, Kade."

Jaycee nodded. "I know the name. He's an FBI agent."

Josh couldn't help but notice that while Jaycee sounded polite, she was eyeing that box.

"Want some?" Bree asked, obviously noticing, too. "Josh sent me a text asking me to pick up a dozen."

"Thanks, both of you." And the moment Bree stepped away, Jaycee grabbed one of the doughnuts and took a huge bite. "Mercy," she mumbled. "That's really good."

And she made a sound of pleasure that had both Grayson and Josh looking at her.

"I'll eat something healthier later," she added.

That wasn't his concern. It was the dab of sugar at the corner of her mouth. Without thinking, Josh reached out, wiped it away and then licked the sugar off his thumb.

He should have given that some thought.

Because even though it'd been an innocent gesture, it sure didn't seem like it.

"All right," Grayson said, rubbing the back of his neck. "I'm going in there to see if he'll spill something. So far, no luck. He keeps insisting that he wants to talk to one of the former hostages."

Grayson left, and Josh continued to read the backgrounds while trying to forget about the sugar-licking episode. Jaycee had a look, too, and continued eating.

"Bryson owns a successful investment company," she pointed out. "Plenty of money to put a baby farm operation together."

Josh tapped Valerie's page. "Ditto for her. She's a prominent attorney. Once served on the city council."

Hardly the profile of someone who would be involved with black-market babies. Still, he'd seen stranger things. And Valerie definitely had the cash to front such a business.

Josh looked up from the pages to see Grayson walking into the interview room. "I'm sorry, but I can't get one of the former hostages here," Grayson explained, sounding very believable.

But Bryson glanced in the mirror. Scowled.

"I doubt that," Bryson grumbled. "You appear to be a resourceful man, but obviously you haven't understood me. I'll only talk to one of the hostages. I need answers to some questions before I'll tell you what I know."

Jaycee huffed. "He's not buying it." She turned to leave. No doubt to go in to the interview room.

Josh caught her arm to stop her. Dropped his gaze to her stomach. "There's a reason you're craving doughnuts, and it's the same reason you should stay put."

She huffed again and turned around to face him. "Look,

we both know I have to do this," she argued. She crammed the rest of the doughnut in her mouth, licked her fingers.

And his body tightened.

Hell. Not now.

What the heck was wrong with him? He was acting like a teenager.

"Are you listening to me?" Jaycee asked.

"Not really."

That answer got her huffing again, but it was the honest truth. He wasn't listening in part because his body was acting crazy, but another part was because he knew what Jaycee was going to say, and he was pretty sure that he wasn't going to like it.

Her hands went on her hips, and the breath she blew out carried her scent. Or rather the sugary sweet scent, thanks to her doughnutfest.

"Both Grayson and you will be in there with me," she argued. "Besides, they were checked for weapons, right?"

They had been. That didn't mean this couldn't get ugly. Jaycee had already been through way too much, and he hated putting her through more. And an interrogation would definitely qualify as *more*.

She lifted his chin. Made eye contact with him. "This could save those women's lives. Heck, it could save *our* lives. Because if we manage to close down the baby farms and arrest those guards, then the danger will be over."

Josh had known this was a battle he was going to lose from the moment he started it, but he'd had to try. A lot was at stake here, and he just wanted to make sure he was thinking straight. He still wasn't certain he was, but he didn't see a lot of options here. They needed Bryson to talk, and he clearly wouldn't start doing that until he laid eyes on Jaycee.

Josh had to make certain that was the only thing Bryson laid on her.

"Don't make me regret this," Josh mumbled.

The relief on her face was instant. Followed by a quick smile. In midsmile she dropped a kiss on his mouth.

Then froze.

"Sorry," Jaycee immediately said. And she winced. "I just got caught up in the moment because I've never won an argument with you. Or maybe it's the sugar high from the doughnut."

Yeah, Josh knew a little about being sorry. The kiss had been hardly more than a peck, but he'd felt it, all right. It must have made him even more stupid, because he started to think about what it would be like to kiss her for real.

Not a peck.

A real kiss.

Even if the past had been settled between them—and it wasn't—he darn sure shouldn't be kissing someone in his protective custody. It was the fastest way to get them both killed.

"Sorry," Josh repeated, and he pulled way back from her. "We've been saying that a lot to each other."

She nodded, and he caught another whiff of her sweet breath when she murmured an agreement. "I think the 'I'm sorrys' are just getting started, though."

He wasn't stupid. Not about this anyway. He figured that applied to many things. The attraction. Her pigheaded views of how to run an investigation. Her views, period. Jaycee and he always seemed to be butting heads, and he was making it worse with this stupid ache he had for her.

Though he hadn't gone through with the kiss, Jaycee must have sensed what he'd been thinking of doing.

"Yeah." She pressed her lips together a moment, and

even though the simple gesture wasn't meant to tease, it made his body tighten again.

And beg.

"It's all right," she added. "I know this attraction doesn't mean anything."

It didn't.

Well, nothing other than he was playing with fire and losing focus. Something that always seemed to happen when he was around Jaycee.

He quickly got that focus back. Josh fired off a text to Grayson to let him know they were about to come in the interview room. Just in case Grayson had any objection. But his cousin only gave a weary nod. Grayson clearly wasn't making any headway with Bryson.

Hoping this wasn't as big a mistake as he figured it was, Josh stayed ahead of Jaycee when they went into the room, but Bryson looked right past Josh. The man barely gave him a glance and then turned to stare at Jaycee.

"I need your help," Bryson said to her, and he slipped his hand inside his jacket, causing both Grayson and Josh to reach for their guns.

Bryson's hand froze for a moment. "It's just a picture," he explained. But Josh and Grayson kept their hands on their guns until Bryson did indeed pull a photograph from his pocket. He held it up for them to see.

"Do you recognize her?" Bryson asked, his attention back on Jaycee. "Was she one of the women being held captive with you at the baby farm?"

Now, that was a question Josh hadn't seen coming. He looked at the photo.

Grayson and Jaycee did, too.

It was a glammed-up shot of a woman in her early thirties, with dark auburn hair that tumbled onto her shoulders. She was wearing a flimsy negligee and a come-hither expression. It was the kind of photo that a woman gave to her lover.

"I don't think she was there," Jaycee said. "Who is she?"

"Sierra DeSilva," Valerie supplied. "My sister."

"She's missing?" Grayson asked.

Valerie lifted her shoulder, and her forehead bunched up. "She could be. Sierra isn't the most responsible person. She often disappears for months at a time. Usually when she has a rich boyfriend who'll cater to her whims." She made a sound of disgust. "And after she's run through all his money, she comes to me looking for more. But this time, she hasn't come back."

Josh intended to do a background check on this Sierra, but first he wanted more information. "Sierra's pregnant?"

"Yes," Bryson and Valerie said in unison. "She should be just about ready to deliver," Bryson added. "And it's my child she's carrying."

"You can't be sure of that," Valerie mumbled.

"I can be," Bryson fired back. That wasn't an affectionate look he was giving Valerie. Or even a civil one. Odd since this woman was his attorney. "I had Sierra take an amnio, and the test proved the child was mine."

"If she didn't have the results faked." Valerie huffed. "You were only with her for a few months. You don't know how manipulative Sierra can be."

Bryson's face reddened, but he didn't challenge that. So maybe Sierra was running some kind of scam and this had nothing to do with the illegal adoptions or baby farms.

Jaycee had another look at the photo. "I remember the faces of the dozen or so women I saw come and go while I was there. But Sierra's face isn't familiar. What makes you think she was one of the captives?"

"This." Bryson reached into his pocket again, but this

time he took out a piece of paper. He put it on the table next to the photo. "It's a ransom demand."

That got Josh's complete attention. To the best of his knowledge, there'd been no demands for any of the other pregnant captives.

None of them touched the letter, but Grayson, Jaycee and Josh leaned closer to have a better look. It was a typed single page, and it had Bryson's name at the top.

"'If you want to see your newborn baby,'" Josh read aloud, "'it'll cost you two hundred grand. Will be in touch tonight with the drop-off details. Don't go to the cops or the deal's off.'"

"I found it on my car windshield yesterday morning," Bryson explained, "but no one's contacted me yet."

Maybe because the operation had been busted the day before when Jaycee and the others had gotten out.

"Is it possible that Sierra was one of the women in the house?" Josh asked Jaycee.

She continued to study the picture. "Maybe. If so, she changed her hair color. All three women in the house were brunettes." Jaycee drew in a weary breath. "But honestly, I didn't get a good look at their faces. The only times that I was in the house were for my weekly checkups, and they didn't let me talk to the other women."

Valerie stood, shoving back the chair so fast that it made a shrill scraping noise on the floor. "I can't sit here and pretend that Sierra's a victim. Because she'd *never* be a victim."

Clearly, Valerie didn't have a high opinion of her sister. Josh needed to run that check on both women ASAP, because something about this didn't feel right.

"You think Sierra's behind the ransom demand?" Grayson asked.

"I do," Valerie said at the same moment Bryson said, "I'm not so sure."

"Bryson's not sure because he wants that to be his child," Valerie snapped. "Because he wants an heir." She pointed at Bryson. "Tell them what Sierra pulled when you broke things off with her. *Tell them,*" she repeated when he didn't answer right away.

Bryson twisted the button on his shirt cuff before he answered. "Sierra and I used to, well, record ourselves when we had sex. She said it was a turn-on. Anyway, after I broke things off with her, she threatened to release the sex tapes if I didn't pay her fifty thousand dollars."

This woman sounded like a real winner. "You paid her?" Josh asked.

"No. I hired someone to break into her place and steal the recordings." His expression turned into a cold glare. "And I'm not apologizing for it, either. My reputation would have been ruined if she'd released them."

"Bryson's married," Valerie supplied. "In name only, but he's married to Elise Wells."

Josh had known the name before he'd ever read Bryson's bio. Bryson's estranged wife wasn't just rich, Elise had powerful friends. Politicians and community business leaders. And yeah, she wouldn't have wanted her husband's sex tapes leaked.

"Any chance your wife had anything to do with the ransom demand?" Grayson wanted to know. "It could be her way of getting back at you."

"Elise isn't involved in this," Bryson said without hesitation.

"But maybe Sierra is," Valerie said the moment Bryson finished. She looked Grayson right in the eyes. "It's possible Sierra's the one who was in charge of that baby farm."

Jaycee and Josh exchanged glances. "Any proof of that?" Josh pressed.

"Only her past behavior. I figure Sierra was plenty angry when she didn't get the blackmail money from Bryson. That's about the time she drained the rest of her trust fund, and I think she did it to set up this operation."

Josh looked at Bryson to see what he thought of this, but the man certainly didn't deny it.

"Find Sierra and the baby," Bryson said, standing. "If she's guilty, put her in jail, but the child is mine."

Grayson stepped in front of the man before he could leave. "If you get another ransom demand, I want to know about it."

Bryson stared at him, the muscles stirring in his jaw, and he finally nodded. "Just don't do anything to endanger that baby."

Bryson left both the photo and the ransom demand on the table and walked out. Valerie started after him, but then stopped right in front of Jaycee.

"If Sierra contacts you for any reason, don't believe a word she says." And with that not-so-sisterly warning, Valerie left, too.

"I'll bag the ransom letter," Grayson said the moment she was gone. "Doubt we'll get anything from it, though, since it was in Bryson's pocket."

Josh agreed, but it was still something that should be done. Grayson left to get the evidence bag, but Jaycee and he stayed put, staring at the photo.

"This baby seems awfully important to Bryson," she commented.

Yeah, and Bryson hadn't talked about his love for the child, so maybe something else was going on. Josh fired off a text to his cousin, FBI agent Kade Ryland, and asked him to do some digging into Bryson's background and marriage.

"So Bryson could be a suspect," Jaycee concluded. "What exactly was there about him in the laptop recovered from the baby farm?"

"No mention of a ransom demand or a connection to a possible captive, that's for sure. It appeared to be some kind of payment to Bryson."

"Payment *to* him?" she questioned.

"Or it could be a falsified payment to make him look guilty. Grayson didn't want to bring it up yet until we know exactly what it is. We didn't want to give Bryson time to come up with some kind of explanation before we spring it on him. If he lies, then we'll have cause to arrest him."

She made a sound to indicate she was giving that some thought. "Any way to match it to money deposited into his account?"

"Accounts," Josh corrected. "The man has dozens of them. We got the court order to look at them, but it's going to take a while to go through all of them."

And that was time that Josh didn't want to spend with Jaycee standing around the sheriff's office. Yes, they had three lawmen in the place, but he preferred her at the ranch where someone couldn't just come walking in the door.

Like those three guards who'd escaped.

Josh motioned for her to follow him down the hall and toward the back exit where he'd parked. "I need to apologize," he said, keeping his voice low so they wouldn't be overheard.

She didn't ask the reason for the latest apology, which meant she knew he was talking about that near kiss. Jaycee only nodded. "Our bodies are having a hard time remembering we're enemies."

Not good. One of them should be sane about this. And

besides, they weren't enemies. He was just having a hard time forgiving her.

The baby was helping with that.

Hard to be angry at the woman carrying his child.

"Call me if you find out anything," Josh told Grayson, and Jaycee and he headed out.

As he'd done on the trip in, Josh checked the parking lot and Main Street to see if there was anyone or anything suspicious, but it looked like a normal weekday in Silver Creek. Still, he hurried to get Jaycee into the truck, and then drove away. However, he'd gone less than a half mile when his phone rang.

It was Grayson. And that meant something big had probably come up for him to call so soon. Even though it could be something neither of them wanted to hear, he decided to put the call on speaker.

"I just talked to Nate," Grayson said the moment Josh answered.

"That's Grayson's brother," Josh explained to Jaycee. "Nate's a lieutenant with the San Antonio P.D."

"Yeah. And he had some info on Bryson," Grayson continued. "Get this—talk around town is that Bryson needs an heir to collect the rest of his family fortune, and his wife is infertile."

"Well, that explains why Bryson wanted the baby." Josh shook his head. "But it doesn't explain his relationship with Sierra. Certainly, someone with his bank accounts could have found someone more reliable to give birth to his child."

"You'd think," Grayson agreed. "Nate's checking into the possibility that Bryson hired Sierra as a surrogate. Maybe one connected to the black-market baby operation."

"And that's why Bryson's name would have been in the

laptop," Jaycee concluded. "However, it doesn't explain why someone at the baby farm would be paying Bryson."

Josh was about to agree, but something caught his attention. A dark blue van. He'd noticed it and four other vehicles trickling by on Main Street when he'd pulled out of the parking lot.

Now it was two cars behind him.

"Is something wrong?" Jaycee said, obviously noticing his glances in the rearview mirror. She turned in the seat to look, too.

"It's probably nothing." Josh took the turn toward the ranch. The car immediately behind him went straight, but the van turned.

So maybe it was really something.

"I need you to run a license plate." And Josh relayed the numbers to Grayson.

Waited.

He tried to give Jaycee a reassuring look, but was certain he failed. After everything she'd been through, he doubted a mere look was going to reassure her of anything anyway. Her breathing had already kicked up, and the pulse was jumping on her throat.

"Where are you?" Grayson said several moments later.

"Just outside of town, about ten miles from the ranch. Why?"

"I'm sending someone your way now, and I'll alert everyone at the ranch." Grayson's words were rushed together. "Because the license plate is fake."

Chapter Eight

"Fake," Jaycee repeated under her breath.

Not just switched plates, but ones that someone had created with bogus numbers so the cops couldn't identify who owned the vehicle. She doubted it was a coincidence that a van with fake plates would just happen to be heading toward the Ryland ranch at the same time as Josh and her.

"Slide down lower in the seat," Josh instructed.

She did, but Jaycee also opened the glove compartment and took out the Colt revolver. Beside her, Josh drew his weapon, too. That didn't help steady her nerves, but Jaycee knew it was necessary.

"I can't turn around," he told her. "The road's too narrow."

Yes, and he'd have to slow down to even attempt it. Right now, the van was keeping a safe distance behind them, and maybe it'd stay like that all the way to the ranch.

Jaycee lifted her head just enough to look in the side mirror so she could try to see who was in the van. The windows were heavily tinted, but she waited until the sunlight speared through some clouds. She could only see shadows, but that was enough.

"There are two people in the front seat," she said. Of course, there could be others in the back.

Sweet heaven.

Were these the guards who'd escaped?

If so, they'd likely come either to kidnap her and take her back to a baby farm or kill her because they didn't want her using any info she might have learned about them. Either way, she'd put Josh right in the middle of this.

And he might not be ready for it.

Josh was suffering from PTSD. She was sure of that. But Jaycee had no idea how that would affect them if they came under a full attack with someone actually shooting at them at close range. Heck, she had no idea how it would affect *her*. She wasn't the agent she used to be, and the baby had to come first. She had to protect her child, and that meant protecting herself.

"The turn's just ahead," Josh pointed out. "We're about five miles from the ranch now."

Five miles might as well be a million if the people in that van were out to attack them. Still, with each passing second, they got closer to the ranch where there would be backup. Plus, Grayson had someone on the way coming from the opposite direction. Both measures might be needed.

Without warning, the van sped up, the tires squealing on the asphalt. And it would have crashed right into them if Josh hadn't sped up, too. Josh cursed and corrected the steering wheel to keep them in their lane.

The van sped up again.

Josh couldn't go any farther to the right because there was a deep ditch filled with water from the spring rains. The tires would just bog up and make them sitting ducks. The only option they had was to continue ahead and hope they made it to the ranch before things went from bad to worse.

"Stay down," Josh reminded her.

Just as the van moved into the oncoming lane.

Jaycee dropped down even farther, but she shifted the gun into position so she could shoot if necessary.

Her heart slammed against her ribs when the van was dead even with them. The side window had a dark tint. Too dark for her to see inside. She braced herself for the passenger to lower the window so he could shoot into the truck.

But he didn't.

The van sped ahead of them, as if it was just passing them, and then it moved back into the right lane.

Jaycee blew out the breath that she'd been holding and glanced at Josh. He had a fierce grip on both the steering wheel and his gun, and his attention was still pinned to the van.

"Call Grayson," Josh instructed, giving her his phone.

"Are you two all right?" Grayson asked the moment he answered.

"So far." She put the call on speaker.

The van remained at a steady speed ahead of them, and even though it was menacing because of those bogus plates, this could turn out to be nothing. Maybe someone with criminal intentions that didn't involve them or just some kind of mix-up with the plates at the DMV.

And Jaycee desperately wanted to believe that.

"Mason's on the way from town," Grayson continued. "Dade's on the way from the ranch. Both should be there soon."

She didn't know who Dade was, but she figured it was another Ryland brother, since there were six of them and they were all lawmen. Jaycee ended the call with Grayson and felt the minutes and the miles click off in her head.

Nothing happened.

But that didn't last long.

Just ahead, she saw the flash of brake lights on the van. It slowed, and Josh followed suit, slowing, too. And then the driver of the van slammed on his brakes, turning the vehicle until it was sideways on the road.

Directly in front of them.

Josh cursed, hit his brakes as well and gave the steering wheel a hard turn to the right. They went into a skid.

It felt as if everything was moving in slow motion. But it was fast, too. It all happened in the blink of an eye. Josh's truck kept moving closer and closer, and Jaycee braced herself for the collision that would crush Josh against the side of the van.

But somehow, Josh managed to stop the truck just inches from the other vehicle.

Jaycee didn't have time to feel any relief.

The new position put them window to window with the van. It would be the perfect time for anyone inside to start shooting. Josh couldn't drive to the left, right or straight ahead. But he threw his truck into Reverse and slammed his foot on the accelerator, speeding away from the vehicle.

Now the van window came down, and she caught a glimpse of the armed man inside, who was wearing a mask. He lifted his gun. Aimed.

Not at her.

But at Josh.

However, Josh ducked to the side just as the bullet slammed into the windshield. The blast tore a gaping hole in the glass. But even over the roar of the blast, she heard a welcome sound.

Sirens.

They were coming from the direction of town, which meant Mason was nearly there. She prayed he got there in time to stop this attack.

The driver of the van no doubt heard the sirens, too. He turned the vehicle and came right at them. No shots. But while Josh continued to drive in Reverse, he took aim through the hole in his windshield, and he fired. Not once but three times. The noise was deafening, and when Jaycee felt the baby kicking, she put her hands over her stomach to try to muffle the sounds.

Jaycee heard the squeal of brakes and glanced over the dash to see the van come to a stop. There were holes in their windshield, too, so maybe Josh had managed to hit the driver.

But she rethought that.

This part of the road was wider, and the van turned around right in the middle, clipping the ditch. The left tires barely missed going into the boggy water. And the moment the driver had the vehicle facing away from the truck, he put the pedal to the metal.

No!

They were getting away.

IT TOOK EVERYTHING inside Josh not to go after those men in the van. They'd clearly tried to kill him, and in doing so, they had endangered Jaycee and the baby. He wanted to beat both of them to a pulp for doing that and then arrest them so he could force the answers out of them about the location of those missing women and the baby farms.

But going after them would put Jaycee at further risk.

Josh had no choice but to stop his truck and ease onto the narrow shoulder. The first thing he did was look at Jaycee to make sure she was okay. She was pale and shaking, her hands still covering her stomach, but she was unharmed.

Well, physically anyway.

This would be another set of images to add to the nightmares she was already having.

Josh looked in his rearview mirror and saw Mason approaching in the cruiser. The blue lights were whirling, and the noise got louder until he came to a stop beside the truck.

"There are at least two of them," Josh relayed. He tipped his head to the windshield. "They're obviously armed."

"Grayson's right behind me. Get Jaycee back to the ranch," Mason said, and he took off after the van.

Josh figured if anyone could catch those men, it'd be Mason, and since he couldn't help his cousin, he threw his truck into gear and started driving.

"You think that man who fired at us was one of the escaped guards?" Josh asked.

Jaycee nodded, brushed some of the pellets of safety glass off her lap and sat up. "Hard to tell, but I'm betting it was."

Yeah, he would bet that, too. Except maybe if this operation was as big as the laptop files led them to believe, then there was no telling how many guards there were.

And how many more attacks there would be.

"These guys seem hell-bent on getting you back. But why?" Josh pressed, though he didn't expect Jaycee to have the answer.

"It can't be something as simple as they don't want me spilling anything about their operation. If it was just that, why aim at you? Why not just kill me?"

The thought of that turned his stomach. But it was a valid question. The guards had likely wanted him out of the picture so they could take Jaycee alive, force her to be a captive again and then steal the baby once she'd delivered.

Josh was trying to deal with that thought when he saw Dade just ahead. His cousin was in his own truck, but it had a portable siren attached, and he slowed as Josh's truck approached him.

"Mason's in pursuit, going west of the farm road," Josh explained to Dade.

"I'm headed there now." And that was the only thing Dade took the time to say before his truck went racing after his brother.

Jaycee gently rubbed her hands over her stomach. It was a soothing motion, but it didn't seem to be working. She looked ready to lose it.

"Maybe the person running the baby farms has a buyer for my baby. Maybe that's why they want me alive." Her voice quivered over the last words.

And Josh's stomach turned again.

He hated the thought of someone using his baby to make money—especially money from a buyer who had heaven knows what in mind when it came to adopting a child. That was why he had to stop these guys, and maybe his Ryland cousins would be able to do that.

Before he even got to the cattle gate at the ranch, he saw the armed hands guarding the road. They waved him through and then closed the gate. Of course, someone could still cut through the miles and miles of pasture, but the ranch hands were out there, too. And more were surrounding the main house.

No kids on the playground today. Thank God they were all tucked safely inside.

Josh drove straight to his barn apartment where there was another armed ranch hand nearby, and got Jaycee up the steps as fast as he could.

And the waiting began.

Neither of them sat down. Too many nerves for that. Jaycee started to pace, and Josh just leaned his back against the door and tried not to lose hope. His cousins had to find these men so the threats would stop.

Her pacing continued for several minutes, but then she jerked to a stop, and her gaze flew across the room toward him. "I didn't even think to ask. But did all of this cause you to have flashbacks?"

It had. Some bad ones, too. But Jaycee had enough demons to battle without adding to the mix.

"I'm okay," he settled for saying. Not quite a lie. Not quite the truth, either. Josh tipped his head to her hands that were still on her belly. "What about you? You need to see a doctor?"

"No," she answered the second he finished the question. "But I think the noise from the shots bothered the baby. It's kicking a lot."

That sent a jolt of concern through him. Josh hadn't even considered something like that. He took out his phone. "I'll call the doctor."

"No," Jaycee repeated, and she made it across the room to him before he could press the numbers. "It's all right, really. The baby's already settling down." And she took his hand and put it on her stomach.

Josh felt a jolt of a different kind. Soft thumps against his hand. For such a small thing, it sure packed an emotional punch. That was his baby in there, moving around and maybe scared from the gunshots.

As he'd seen Jaycee do, he rubbed his hand over the movements. Then he realized what he was doing. It wasn't just his baby he was feeling.

But also Jaycee.

He lifted his head. Met her gaze. There was no fear in her eyes this time, but there was some kind of connection between them because of the baby.

Or maybe it was something else.

After studying her, he was leaning toward the something else.

Jaycee's mouth parted; her breath was slow and warm. Like the look she suddenly got in her eyes. And he caught her scent. Not the sweat and fear from the attack. But something feminine and fiery hot.

Okay, that last one was probably his imagination.

Or wishful thinking.

Because he was suddenly having some fiery-hot thoughts about her.

He could blame it on the adrenaline, but Josh was suddenly in the mood to make another huge mistake. And he dived right in. He slid his hand around the back of her neck and pulled her to him. In the same motion, he put his mouth to hers for a kiss that shouldn't be happening.

He expected Jaycee to push him away. To remind him they shouldn't be doing this.

She didn't.

Jaycee made a sound. A soft moan of pleasure, and she slipped her arms around his neck. Worse, she kissed him right back.

Part of this had to be the shot of fear they'd just had from the attack and all that touching he'd done on her stomach. But he was pretty sure the bulk of the kiss was just about the fire that'd always been between them. Josh made that fire a whole lot worse by deepening the kiss.

Jaycee did her own share of deepening, and she eased her body against him. Because of her pregnant belly, it wasn't possible for them to get as close as he wanted. But, man, did they try. And what had started out as a stupid, really good kiss ended with a bad ache inside him.

She pulled back. Their eyes met again. And he saw the urgent need there for just a split second before they went at each other again. This kiss was deeper and hotter than the first. As if they were starved for each other.

Maybe they were.

Josh hadn't been with a woman since Jaycee. Not much time for that while recovering from a gunshot wound and jump-starting his life. He doubted Jaycee had been with anyone, either. So, maybe it was just because they needed someone. *Anyone*.

And Josh wished he could believe that.

It would be so much easier than feeling all this fire. This ache. This confusion.

Because it was wrong to kiss Jaycee like this if he couldn't forgive her, and he wasn't certain he was ready to do that.

Josh also got that bad feeling in the back of his head. The one that whispered he might never be able to forgive her. He pulled back. But stayed close.

Her face was flushed, and her breath was ragged. She was looking at him as if they'd lost their minds.

A distinct possibility.

Especially on his part.

"Don't," she said, easing back. "I don't want you to say you're sorry unless you truly are."

Since Josh had no idea if that *truly* applied to him, he just kept his mouth shut and tried to talk himself out of kissing her again.

Yeah, talk about zero willpower.

It took him a few seconds to realize the ringing sound wasn't in his head. It was his phone. Good grief. With everything going on, the last thing he should be doing was kissing Jaycee, since it was a serious distraction. Among other things.

Still cursing himself, Josh took out the phone expecting to see one of his cousin's names. But it was the 911 dispatcher.

"Josh Ryland," he answered, wondering what the heck had gone wrong now.

"Deputy Ryland," the man said, "someone just called

and said it was an emergency, that she needed to speak to you right away. She sounded desperate—"

"Who is it?" Josh asked.

"She won't give me her name, but I can transfer the call to you. You can talk to her yourself." And the seconds crawled by until Josh heard the woman.

"Deputy Ryland?" the woman didn't wait for him to confirm it. "You have to help me. Please."

"Who is this?" he demanded. Jaycee moved closer to the phone so she could hear.

"It's Sierra DeSilva."

Well, he hadn't expected to hear from her. Especially not like this. "I just had a chat with your sister and your ex-lover, Bryson. Did one of them contact you?"

"No. I haven't seen either of them in weeks." She made a hoarse-sounding sob. "I was kidnapped and taken to some kind of place where they're holding pregnant women."

Everything inside Josh went still. "A baby farm?"

"Yes," Sierra jumped to say. "And I just escaped. Please, Deputy Ryland, come and get me. Because if they find me, they'll kill me."

Chapter Nine

Jaycee was back to pacing again. This time at the Silver Creek sheriff's office while she waited for Josh and the other deputies to return with Sierra. Josh had insisted she not go with Grayson, Dade and him to collect the woman.

Because it could be a trap.

So instead Josh had taken her to the sheriff's office, where she was being guarded by yet two more of his cousins. Gage and Bree. According to what Josh had told her, both had once worked for the Justice Department and had loads of training.

And they were a vigilant pair.

Even though Jaycee couldn't see her from the office doorway, Bree was posted at the rear exit, armed and ready for a possible attack. Gage was at the front door. They'd given Jaycee strict orders to stay away from the windows.

Which she'd done.

She wanted Sierra rescued safe and sound. If the woman truly needed rescuing, that was. But Jaycee didn't want to be part of the rescue if it meant putting her own baby at further risk.

If Sierra contacts you for any reason, don't believe a word she says, Valerie had warned them.

But the problem with that was Jaycee didn't know if they could trust Valerie, either. This could be a case of bad blood between siblings, and maybe Sierra was innocent in all of this.

Maybe.

Or this could be some kind of hoax meant to draw out Josh for another attempt to kill him.

She looked up at the clock on the wall again. Frowned. Not even a minute had passed since she'd last checked, and since she couldn't tamp down all this pressure-cooker energy inside her, she just kept pacing.

It'd only been forty minutes since Josh and the others had left to get Sierra at an abandoned gas station just outside of town. That wasn't nearly enough time to start worrying that something had gone wrong.

But Jaycee worried anyway.

She blamed that in part on that stupid kiss. It'd been wonderful, no doubt about it, but that didn't make it right. Josh still had to deal with his feelings for her. Added to that, they needed to focus on the case. However, that wasn't even the best reason to ban all future kissing.

It was because she was falling for him.

Of course, she'd had a thing for Josh since she'd first met him several years ago, but that kiss had reminded her that the *thing* could be a whole lot more. She needed to nip that idiotic notion in the bud and not weave some stupid fantasy of them getting together to be a family.

Besides, she didn't want a family. She'd had one of those once, and it hadn't worked out so well.

She only wanted for her baby to be safe.

The bell jangled over the front door and Jaycee peered out from the office. She saw Grayson come in. Then Dade, who had his arm looped around a pale-skinned woman with flaming red hair.

Sierra, no doubt.

The woman was indeed pregnant and had her hands splayed over her stomach.

As good as it was to see that Sierra had been rescued, Jaycee didn't stop holding her breath until Josh walked in. Her heart did a flip-flop. And she cursed it. Because she figured her heart shouldn't continue to have a say in this.

It'd rarely made good decisions in the past.

Josh snagged her gaze for just a second and she could see the relief in his eyes. Relief no doubt because there'd been no repeat attacks while he was gone. They all moved toward Grayson's office, but Gage kept his position at the door, probably to make sure Sierra and the others hadn't been followed.

"You have to find her," Sierra said, her breath ragged.

"Her?" Jaycee asked.

"The woman who escaped with me. I don't know her name, but we both sneaked out of the house when the guard was asleep."

"Any sign of this woman?" Jaycee asked.

Josh shook his head. "Sierra said they got separated in the woods."

"We did," Sierra verified, frantically bobbing her head. "And this woman isn't well. In fact, I think she's crazy. Doesn't surprise me after being held in that horrible place. Anyway, she was rambling, saying things that didn't make sense."

Yes, it would be easy to lose your mind while being held captive, and Jaycee hated the thought of this woman wandering around in the woods.

"We'll find her," Josh insisted, and the other Rylands voiced some kind of agreement.

"We'll keep Sierra here for a little while," Grayson explained to Jaycee. "There were two suspicious vehicles with out-of-state plates in the parking lot at the hospital, so I thought it'd be safer to bring her here."

That got Jaycee's heart pounding. Those armed guards could be in the vehicles. They could come to the sheriff's office and stage another attack to kill Josh.

Josh must have seen the worry in her eyes because he ran his hand over Jaycee's arm. "It's okay. Mason and the other deputy are checking out the vehicles now."

"It's someone looking for me," Sierra concluded, her voice filled with nerves.

No one in the room disputed that.

Jaycee and Josh moved back so Dade could ease Sierra onto the small leather sofa in Grayson's office. Dade got her a bottle of water, then excused himself, saying he needed to go help Mason and the deputy deal with those vehicles.

Sierra had a hefty sip of water before the tears came spilling down her cheeks. "I can't believe I got away from them. They'll come for me," she added in a broken whisper.

"Where were you when you escaped?" Jaycee asked.

Sierra looked at her as if she hadn't noticed her before in the room despite Jaycee asking her a question earlier. "I'm not sure. I've already told the sheriff that it was about a mile or so from the gas station. I stole a phone before I got away, but there wasn't any service until I actually got to the gas station."

"There are a lot of dead spots for cell phones out there," Grayson added. "But we've called the Texas Rangers so they can comb the area."

"They have to find it," Sierra said. "There are other women being held captive."

It sickened Jaycee to hear that, but if Sierra was telling the truth, those women stood a good chance of being rescued tonight.

"Your sister came in earlier," Josh tossed out there. "And Bryson."

At the mention of those names, Sierra's tears dried up and her mouth tightened. "Let me guess. They had all sorts of lies to tell about me." Not exactly a question.

Josh lifted his shoulder. "Bryson said you tried to blackmail him over some sex tapes."

Sierra didn't blush, didn't even dodge his intense lawman's stare. "I simply asked him to pay me for the tapes. Did he also tell you that he broke into my place to get them?"

Josh nodded. "If you want to file charges against him, I'll put you in contact with someone at SAPD."

"That's water under the bridge." Sierra got that distressed look again as if she might start crying. "I'm the victim here. Not my money-grubbing sister and my ex-boyfriend. In fact, you should look at both of them, because either of them could be behind these baby farms."

Great. The sisters had now accused each other of running this heinous business. "You have any proof that they're responsible?" Jaycee pressed.

Sierra quickly nodded. "I do. I have some of Valerie's bank records at my apartment. They prove that she was withdrawing huge sums of money from her trust fund."

Grayson and Josh exchanged glances. "How'd you get these records?" Grayson asked.

Now Sierra's gaze darted away. "I saw them in her office and copied them, all right? I knew she was up to no good, and I wanted some proof."

So she'd stolen them. And tried to use a sex tape to extort money from her former lover. Sierra definitely had some credibility issues, but at least she didn't seem to be dodging their questions.

"Does your sister need money or something?" Josh

pressed. "I ask because I'm just wondering why you'd think she would do this."

"Money, definitely," Sierra said. "Yes, she's got plenty of it, but she'd love to have much more. With Valerie it's always more, more, more, and she doesn't care who she steps on to get it."

Obviously, they needed to take a hard look at Valerie's financials. Of course, this could all be lies. Or not. Sierra certainly seemed shaken, but Jaycee had to admit that it could all be an act.

Sierra gave a weary sigh. "I know it's hard to think this about one's own sister, but I believe Valerie could have had me kidnapped so she could sell my baby to Bryson."

Interesting.

Jaycee couldn't completely dismiss that theory. From everything she'd seen, Bryson would indeed pay a huge ransom to get his heir. Of course, Bryson himself could be behind this, too. He could have had Sierra kidnapped to ensure that he got his hands on the baby.

So now they had three suspects.

Sierra, Bryson and Valerie.

Jaycee didn't have a gut feeling about any of them except that she didn't intend to trust any of them.

"Can someone call Bryson and tell him I've been rescued?" Sierra asked.

The request was a surprise, considering that minutes earlier she'd accused him of telling lies about her.

"I can call him," Grayson finally said, though he sounded as suspicious as Jaycee felt. "Anything specific you want me to tell him?"

"Yes. Tell him if he cares about this baby at all, he'll get his butt down here to Silver Creek right away or he'll never see his child." But Sierra waved that off and sniffled again. "It's just the nerves talking."

Sierra paused, gathered her breath. "Bryson cut me to the core when I told him I was pregnant. I wanted him to divorce his cold fish of a wife and marry me. But he refused."

Of course he did. His rich wife gave him the standing in the community that he wanted. But what about that standing once everyone learned he'd cheated on his wife and gotten another woman pregnant? He might collect his inheritance but could lose everything else.

Grayson's phone rang, and he glanced at the screen. "It's Mason," he told them, and answered it. "What'd you find out about those suspicious vehicles?"

Jaycee couldn't hear what Mason said, but the call was short. Grayson ended it and looked at Sierra. "False alarm on the vehicles. Some kids on a class trip got food poisoning, and this was the nearest hospital. Come on. I'll take you to see the doctor."

Sierra didn't argue. She wobbled a little when she stood and touched her hand to her head. "Someone please call Bryson and tell him what I've been through."

"I will," Josh assured her.

"Tell him to come to the hospital," Sierra added. "I need to see him."

Josh just nodded, and they watched as Grayson took her by the arm and led her back out to the squad car.

"You believe her?" Jaycee asked.

Josh shrugged. "I believe she's a gold digger, and that means I automatically distrust her."

Yes, so did she. Besides, Sierra was giving off mixed signals about Bryson. In one breath she was bad-mouthing him, and in the next she wanted to see him. Of course, she could have wanted to see him just to try to get money out of him. Still, that seemed a strange reaction considering the ordeal she'd just been through.

Josh located Bryson's contact number in Grayson's files, and he made the call. "No answer," he muttered after letting it ring a half dozen times, and he left a message for the man to contact him ASAP.

"What about Valerie's financials?" Jaycee asked.

Josh nodded, and he fired off a text. This time to his cousin Kade Ryland, who was an FBI agent. He asked not just for info on Valerie but for a search warrant for Sierra's apartment.

"The warrant shouldn't be hard to get," Josh said to her when he finished texting. "We can tie it to her kidnapping and the baby farm investigation."

"Good. And during the search maybe they'll run across those bank statements that Sierra said she had. If not, I figure Sierra would gladly hand them over since they seem to implicate her sister of some wrongdoing. Or not," Jaycee quickly added.

"Yeah. This could be just a bad case of sibling rivalry."

He checked the time and tipped his head to the door. "Ready to get out of here? I can have Gage or Bree escort us back to the ranch."

Jaycee hated to tie up so much manpower just to protect her and now Sierra. However, after what'd happened on their last drive to the ranch, she welcomed the extra security.

"Let me get everything ready," Josh said, but he didn't even make it a step before his phone rang.

Jaycee expected it to be Bryson returning his call, but she saw *emergency dispatcher* on the screen.

"Deputy Ryland," Josh answered. And since he didn't put the call on speaker, Jaycee moved close enough to hear. She prayed this wasn't yet more bad news.

"There's another woman trying to contact you," the dispatcher told Josh. "She says her name is Miranda Culley and that it's important. Could be some kind of prank—"

"I'll talk to her," Josh interrupted. "You know her?" he mouthed to Jaycee.

But she had to shake her head.

"Deputy Ryland?" the woman said the moment Josh answered. "I heard them say your name so that's why I asked for you." Her breath was gusting and her words rushed together. "I knew it was safe to call you. Because I figure if they want you dead, then you're not working for them."

"Who wants me dead?" Josh asked.

"The guards." A sob tore from her throat. "Four months ago I was kidnapped. And I gave birth to my baby yesterday. The guards took her. I don't know where. But they were going to kill me, and I managed to escape. I can't look for my baby on my own. I need your help."

Oh, mercy. This didn't sound good at all.

"Escaped from where?" Josh pressed.

"A ranch out in the middle of nowhere. I need your help, please," she repeated. "And I need you to find my baby and arrest the person who did this to us."

The muscles in his jaw turned to iron. "You know who the person is?"

"I know." The woman made another ragged sound.

And the line went dead.

Chapter Ten

"Miranda?" Josh repeated, though he knew it was useless. The call had ended, and he didn't know if the woman had done that herself or if someone else was responsible for the disconnection.

Josh immediately phoned back the dispatcher. "What's the number Miranda Culley was calling from?"

"It's from a prepaid cell phone."

Josh groaned. There was no way to trace that, but it did make him wonder where she'd gotten the burner. Maybe like Sierra, she'd stolen it from one of the guards.

"If she calls back, put her straight through to me," Josh instructed.

"You know her?" Josh asked Jaycee when he ended the call with the dispatcher.

"No." Jaycee shook her head and moved to Grayson's laptop. "I'll check NCIC."

The National Crime Information Center was a database for missing persons. It was a good start, but it'd be even better if Miranda called back and told them where the heck she was.

And if she gave them the name of the person responsible.

They needed that info from Miranda so they could make

an arrest and put an end to not just the baby farms but the attacks, as well.

"She's missing, all right," Jaycee confirmed several moments later. "Miranda Ann Culley is twenty-eight, single and worked as a waitress in Kerrville. No immediate family, but her boss reported her missing two months ago."

"No mention of the father of her baby?"

Another head shake and more clicks on the computer keyboard. "She does have a record, though. Busted for drugs six years ago. Nothing since."

So she'd cleaned herself up. Maybe. Or maybe she just hadn't gotten caught. And that led Josh to something else he had to consider. "This could be a setup to lure us out into the open."

Jaycee met his gaze from over the top of the computer. "Sierra wasn't a setup." She paused, groaned softly. "I don't want it to be a setup. If she was held captive like I was, then I want her rescued."

Survivor's guilt. Something Josh recognized because he felt it himself. His partner, Ben, had died, and he hadn't. It didn't matter that he'd had no say in the matter as to who had lived and who had died. Jaycee hadn't had a say in her captivity and rescue, either.

But the guilt was still there.

"I want all of them rescued," Jaycee added. Her voice trembled, and she cursed. "Damn hormones."

He suspected the hormones weren't nearly as much to blame as the guilt and Jaycee's need to get justice for all the women who'd been taken. Josh went to her, knowing it was a mistake to get this close when the emotions were sky-high. It was also a mistake to put his arms around her.

But he did it anyway.

"When you're nice to me, it only makes it harder," Jaycee mumbled.

He eased back, looked at her and his eyebrow lifted, questioning that.

"If you're angry with me," she said, her voice barely a whisper now, "then I can forget about that night we spent together."

His eyebrow lifted higher.

"All right, so maybe I can't forget it entirely," Jaycee amended. "But I can focus on the anger and nothing else."

Nothing else as in the heat.

It'd been the overwhelming need for each other that had sent them racing to bed five months earlier. No finesse. No foreplay. Just the fire that had given them no choice. Well, no choice that they'd wanted to take anyway. At the time, Josh hadn't thought there'd be huge consequences, like a pregnancy.

He had definitely been wrong about that.

"You want me to yell at you?" he joked. And it surprised him that he could make light of something like that. Two days ago, he would have shut her out with his anger and his words.

The kisses had changed everything.

And he added to the change by kissing her again.

Oh, man. He was in big trouble here.

There was no way he should feel what he was feeling. It wasn't right. Logical. Or any other label he could put on it. But did that stop him?

Nope.

He just kissed her as if the world around them wasn't a giant powder keg that could explode at any moment. Josh might have kept kissing Jaycee for hours if he hadn't felt the movement. The soft thuds against his stomach.

"The baby's kicking," Jaycee whispered, her mouth still on his.

Josh slid his hand between them and over the kicks. It

felt like a rodeo going on in there, and he chuckled before he realized he was even going to do it.

Jaycee pulled back, looking a little stunned. "I've never heard you laugh before."

Josh was about to say that was impossible, but it had been a while since he'd let himself feel anything close to laughter.

More survivor's guilt.

His dead partner, Ben, couldn't laugh anymore. Couldn't live. So Josh had shut down, too. The problem was that he didn't know how to start back up again. How to forget that Jaycee had been responsible for that attack.

How to forgive.

And it was that reminder that had him pulling away from her. "Sorry."

He could have added more—exactly what, he didn't know—but his phone rang again. Josh snatched it up, hoping to see the 911 operator with Miranda's return call, but it was Grayson.

"We've got a problem," Grayson said the second that Josh answered.

Josh groaned and put the call on speaker so he wouldn't have to repeat the bad news to Jaycee.

"Sierra sneaked out of the hospital," Grayson added. "She told us she had to go to the bathroom, but she's gone. She left a note on the mirror saying that she wasn't sure she could trust us, that she thought one of us would hand her back over to the kidnappers."

Josh cursed. This wasn't just frustrating, it was downright dangerous for Sierra and her baby. Didn't Sierra realize that?

"I doubt she'll come to the sheriff's office," Josh said. "You have someone out looking for her?"

"Yeah, and I'm about to join them. Just thought you should know that Valerie and Bryson are headed your way."

Really? He didn't need this now. "Why?"

"I contacted Bryson just as Sierra wanted, and he said he was on the way. Just called him back though to say she'd left, but Valerie and he were already en route. Bryson insisted on going to the sheriff's office to wait for any news about Sierra."

Of course he would. He wanted to get his hands on that baby, and Sierra was due any time now.

"If Jaycee's holding up all right," Grayson said, "then you two stay put awhile longer with Gage and Bree."

"Will do." But the words had no sooner left Josh's mouth when he heard the jangle of the front doorbell. He also heard Valerie's and Bryson's voices before he even glanced out of the office and into the reception area.

"How could you possibly let her get away?" Bryson demanded of Gage, who'd been standing guard.

"You're looking at the wrong guy," Gage drawled, and then proceeded to frisk them, despite protests from the two. "They aren't armed," he relayed to Josh.

With his gun still drawn, Gage stepped just outside the door and looked around. No doubt to see if the pair had been followed or if they had brought any hired guns with them.

"No one *let* Sierra get away," Josh informed Bryson. "She lied to the sheriff so she could slip out of the hospital." Something he was sure Grayson had already told the man.

"Someone let her sneak out," Bryson argued. "She should have been watched the entire time."

"She wasn't under arrest," Josh fired back. But clearly she'd been a flight risk, something none of them had picked up on. Everything Sierra had said led Josh to believe that she wanted to be rescued. And maybe she still did. She just didn't trust them to do the rescuing.

"Oh, God," Bryson mumbled. He touched his fingers to his mouth. "What if those kidnappers took her again and made it look as if she'd left on her own?"

Josh couldn't totally discount that, but it wasn't adding up to another kidnapping. Grayson would have told him if there'd been any sign of a struggle or if Sierra had called out for help. Neither of those things had happened.

Valerie frowned. "My sister's clever, and if she'd wanted to leave, no one would have stopped her. She would have found a way." Valerie's attention went to Jaycee when she stepped into the hall. "Good, I'm glad you're here. It saves me from tracking you down."

"What do you want?" Jaycee asked, and her tone matched both Valerie's and Bryson's—unfriendly.

"You must remember something about your time as a captive. A name, a face. A place. Anything that would help us get to the bottom of this and find out who might have taken my sister."

Jaycee shook her head. "I've told Josh and the sheriff everything I remember, and it's nothing that would help find Sierra." She looked at Josh, lowered her voice to a whisper. "I think it's time to ask him about what the tech found on the laptop."

Josh stayed quiet a moment, then nodded. "Care to explain why your name was found on a computer recovered from the baby farm?" Josh came right out and asked the man.

"Probably because Sierra told them he was the rich father of her baby," Valerie said before Bryson could answer. "And she would have done that so they could force Bryson to pay up after she delivered."

Bryson huffed. What he didn't do was look surprised at

the revelation that he had a connection to the baby farm. He came out of the reception area and into the hall, but he stopped several yards away. "I just want to find Sierra before she has the baby and does something stupid like try to sell it."

"From everything you've told me about her, Sierra will offer the baby to you first," Josh reminded him. "I don't think you have to worry about her going to a stranger." Unless Bryson didn't pay up, that is. Or maybe Bryson was concerned that someone would pay more than he was willing to.

"What if these guards don't give her a choice?" Bryson pressed.

"Then I'm sure you'll hear about it." Because he was pretty sure the bottom line here was still all about the money. "What I don't understand is why the computer record showed that someone from the baby farm had sent you money."

Now Bryson had a reaction. "Impossible!" he howled. "There's no way I'd accept money from snakes like that. Besides, I don't need money."

On the surface, that was true. "Maybe it was a way of taking care of Sierra. The person running the baby farm could have paid you when you turned Sierra over to them. That way she couldn't run, and if the baby turned out to be yours, then you could always buy it and not have to deal with Sierra."

"That's despicable." Bryson's eyes narrowed. "And if you repeat idiotic lies like that, you'll be facing a lawsuit for defamation."

Valerie caught on to her client to keep him from going closer to Josh. "I'm sure we'll get all of this sorted out once we find my sister."

Josh wasn't so sure of that. Sierra hadn't been able to

give them much info that would lead them back to the person running the baby farm.

Both Bryson and Valerie started throwing questions at him again. Questions about how he intended to find Sierra and what he'd do with her once she was back in protective custody. Josh had no intention of giving them info like that, and besides, he wanted both of them out of there.

"My advice is for both of you to go back to your homes in case Sierra turns up at one of them."

Valerie and Bryson stopped their string of questions, and Valerie whispered something to Bryson that Josh didn't catch because his phone rang again.

Finally. It was the emergency dispatcher.

"I have to take this call," Josh said to their visitors.

He didn't wait for the two to respond. Jaycee and he stepped back into Grayson's office and Josh closed the door before he hit the answer button.

"It's that woman, Miranda Culley, again," the dispatcher said, and put the call through.

"Are you all right?" Josh immediately asked with the call on speaker.

"I had to hang up because I thought I heard footsteps coming toward me. I had to move. I'd stolen one of the guard's phones, and I was worried they'd be able to trace it somehow."

Again, she'd dodged his question. That didn't make Josh trust her, but he was still hoping she had critical information that could make Jaycee and countless others finally feel safe.

"You need to tell me where you are and who's responsible for the baby farm," Josh demanded.

"I will, but first I want to speak to Agent Jaycee Finney."

Everything inside Josh went still. Jaycee had already

said she didn't know the woman, so why did Miranda know her name?

"Why her?" Josh pressed when Miranda didn't continue.

"Because I heard the guards talking about her, too. They want her baby, but she escaped. I think that means I can trust her, that she isn't working for those guards."

"You can trust me," Jaycee said despite Josh shaking his head for her to stay quiet. He didn't want her involved in this any more than she already was.

"The guards hate you," Miranda said a moment later. "They hate Deputy Ryland, too. That's why I called him. Please tell me that you won't try to kill me when we meet."

Josh had to fight to make sure he didn't snap at her, but the woman was testing his patience. "I have no intention of killing you. I want to help. Just tell me where you are."

Silence.

For a long time.

So long that Josh checked and made sure the call hadn't been disconnected. It hadn't been.

"All right," Miranda finally said. It sounded as if she'd just had a long debate with herself. "There's an old cemetery on Martin Road. You know the place?"

"Yeah." It wasn't that far from the Ryland ranch. "Are you there now?"

"No, but I'll meet you and Jaycee there in two hours."

"Jaycee isn't coming," Josh said before the woman even finished.

Thankfully, Jaycee didn't argue with him, though that was an arguing look she had in her eyes.

"If Jaycee doesn't come, there'll be no meeting," Miranda insisted.

"You'd better come up with a different plan, then," Josh fired back.

There was another snail-crawling silence, and Josh hoped at the end of this one, Miranda would show some common sense. It wouldn't be smart for Jaycee to be out there meeting a captive when the guards were looking to kidnap or do heaven knows what to her again.

"If Jaycee isn't with you," Miranda finally said, "you won't even see me. Because if she's there, I know it won't be some kind of trap."

Josh muttered some profanity. "Then tell me who's behind the baby farms." Yeah, he wanted to rescue Miranda—if she truly needed rescuing, that is—but he didn't want to do that at Jaycee and the baby's expense.

"The only way I'll tell you that is when I'm face-to-face with you and Jaycee. If you want to know the truth, then I'll see you both in two hours."

And with that, Miranda hung up.

"You're not going," Josh said to Jaycee before she could launch into that argument he could still see brewing.

"Hey, get away from there," Gage called out.

Josh threw open the door to see what had caused Gage to say that, but Bryson and Valerie were no longer in the hall. They were right outside the office door.

And judging from their thunderstruck expressions, they'd heard every word about the meeting with Miranda.

Chapter Eleven

"The call wasn't about Sierra," Josh snarled at Bryson and Valerie. "And it's time for both of you to leave."

Jaycee agreed. Josh and she needed to make plans for that meeting with Miranda, and she didn't want to do that with Bryson and Valerie lurking around.

But neither moved despite the fact that Gage was charging right at them.

"You found another hostage," Bryson mumbled. "And this woman knows who took her and the others." He latched on to Josh's arm. "I have to go with you to that meeting. I have to find out who's responsible, because these people might have taken Sierra again."

"No," Gage argued. "What you have to do is leave now. And if you don't, I'll arrest you on the spot."

"You can't do that," Valerie fired back. "This woman might be able to tell us about Sierra."

Gage didn't say another word. He just took out his handcuffs and put Bryson against the wall. Bryson didn't go willingly, and he started to curse. When the man struggled to get away, Gage used his forearm to slam him harder against the wall.

"Stop this!" Valerie yelled.

But Gage didn't stop. Neither did Josh. He also grabbed

FREE Merchandise is 'in the Cards' for you!

Dear Reader,

We're giving away FREE MERCHANDISE!

Seriously, we'd like to reward you for reading this novel by giving you **FREE MERCHANDISE** worth over $20. And no purchase is necessary!

You see the Jack of Hearts sticker above? Paste that sticker in the box on the Free Merchandise Voucher inside. Return the Voucher promptly...and we'll send you valuable Free Merchandise!

Thanks again for reading one of our novels—and enjoy your Free Merchandise with our compliments!

Pam Powers

Pam Powers

P.S. Look inside to see what Free Merchandise is **"in the cards"** for you!

We'd like to send you two free books like the one you are enjoying now. Your two books have a combined price of over $10, but they are yours to keep absolutely FREE! We'll even send you 2 wonderful surprise gifts. You can't lose!

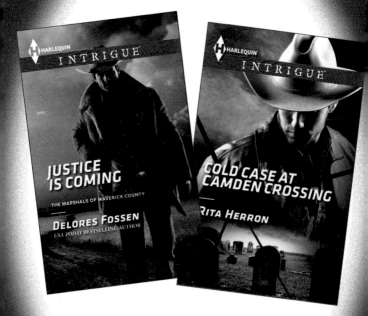

REMEMBER: Your Free Merchandise, consisting of **2 Free Books** and **2 Free Gifts**, is worth over $20.00! No purchase is necessary, so please send for your Free Merchandise today.

Get TWO FREE GIFTS!

We'll also send you two wonderful FREE GIFTS (worth about $10), in addition to your 2 Free books!

Visit us at:
www.ReaderService.com

Detach card and mail today. No stamp needed.

FREE MERCHANDISE VOUCHER

2 FREE
BOOKS
and
2 FREE
GIFTS

Please send my Free Merchandise, consisting of
2 Free Books and **2 Free Mystery Gifts**.
I understand that I am under no obligation to buy
anything, as explained on the back of this card.

❑ I prefer the regular-print edition
182/382 HDL GEEK

❑ I prefer the larger-print edition
199/399 HDL GEEK

Please Print

FIRST NAME

LAST NAME

ADDRESS

APT.#   CITY

STATE/PROV.   ZIP/POSTAL CODE

NO PURCHASE NECESSARY!

HI_314_FM13

some cuffs from the shelf in Grayson's office and went after Valerie.

"Okay, we're leaving," she snapped, holding up her hands in a back-off gesture. "But this isn't over."

Gage didn't stop cuffing Bryson until Josh gave the nod, and when Bryson whirled around to face Josh and her, there was pure venom in his eyes.

"Like Valerie said, this isn't over," Bryson repeated through clenched teeth. "And if you think it is, you're dead wrong."

A chill went through Jaycee. "As far as I'm concerned, your business is finished here," Gage fired back.

The staring match lasted just a few long moments, but Valerie and Bryson finally got moving toward the front door—while they tossed out some profanity. However, Bryson gave them one last glare from over his shoulder. Gage glared back, and he shut and locked the door behind them.

"I'm betting they'll try to follow us to the meeting," Jaycee said.

"Us?" Josh challenged.

Jaycee groaned. Josh was going to give her a hassle about going.

"You heard what Miranda said. She'll only talk to both of us." And because it was important, Jaycee stepped in front of Josh and forced him to look at her so he could hopefully see the determination on her face.

But he only dropped his gaze to her stomach. Josh didn't have to say a word. That little glance was her reminder that going to the meeting could put the baby in danger.

"I'm not stupid. I know it's risky, but together we could minimize the risks and still find Miranda." Hopefully, she'd be safe and ready to spill everything about who was behind the baby farms.

Josh shook his head. "Minimizing the risks still means there'll be risks."

"Heck, it's a risk with me just being here. Or anywhere. The sooner we get answers, the sooner the risks will disappear."

She hoped.

But Jaycee had to admit that an operation like this might have many heads.

Nevertheless, it would feel good to get one of those heads off the street and in jail. And besides, one arrest could lead them to another. Then all of them could come toppling down until they got to the idiot who had orchestrated this operation.

Josh drew in a weary breath and sat down on the edge of the desk. Jaycee thought he was beginning to bend just a little, and she was about to propose a plan, but before she could utter a word of it, Josh's phone rang.

"It's Kade," he said, glancing at the screen.

Kade, his cousin in the FBI. Jaycee really hoped this wasn't bad news and that it'd be a short and sweet conversation, because Josh and she had a lot of details to work out. That included her convincing him that she had to be part of that meeting.

"I've found some interesting stuff on Bryson Hillard," Kade said when Josh answered. "Thought you'd like to know right away."

"I do," Josh assured him, and he checked the time. "Just make it fast. Jaycee and I have a lot on our plate right now." It was still an hour and forty-five minutes until the meeting with Miranda, which didn't give them much time to get ready.

Or for her to convince Josh why she should go.

"We ran the financials on Bryson," Kade started. "No red flags, but we got one from a criminal informant. A reliable one, too. He says Bryson has some gambling debts and he owes money to the wrong people. And that those wrong people are sucking huge weekly payments from him to cover the loan."

Jaycee had to mentally repeat that. "But Bryson's rich," she pointed out.

"Yeah," Kade agreed. "But his wife controls most of the money. It's hers, not his, and she's not keen on shelling out cash for her husband's gambling debts. She gave him his annual allowance at the first of the year. A quarter of a million. But it appears he's already gone through the bulk of that."

Wow, that certainly hadn't come up in any of their conversations, and it got the wheels turning in her head. Especially after she remembered his steely glare and the threat he'd issued just minutes earlier.

"If he's not getting the money from his wife to pay off the gambling debts," Josh asked, "then where's it coming from?"

"Not sure," Kade quickly answered. "He's not pulling it from any of his private accounts. Not enough money in them for that. Of course, he could have some account that he's managed to keep hidden."

That was possible, of course. If he was illegally gambling, then he could have some other illegal way to earn some income.

"What if Bryson is the one who set up the baby farms? He could have used what was left of his yearly allowance to hire the guards and such." Jaycee was thinking out loud now, and she wasn't sure all the facts would add up when she was done.

But sadly, it did make some sense.

Desperate people did desperate things, and he could have gotten the idea for the operation after Sierra told him she was pregnant. By kidnapping her, he could contain Sierra and eventually get the child he needed as an heir, all the while kidnapping other pregnant women.

"He could be paying off the debts with the money he gets from selling the babies," Jaycee added. Which could amount to tens of thousands of dollars.

Both Kade and Josh stayed quiet for several moments, and then Josh nodded. "That would explain why Sierra was taken captive. She was trying to force him to pay for his own baby. This way, he could maybe milk the money from Valerie or even his wife with the promise he'll pay her back when he collects the rest of his inheritance."

And if that was true, then it made Bryson a criminal of the worst sort. He was endangering babies and birth mothers—including his own child—for personal gain.

"There's more," Kade said, bringing their attention back to him. "I found a red flag on Valerie's accounts, too. Her sister was right about all those withdrawals. When the dust settles over there, you'll probably want to bring her in and ask her about them."

She really didn't want to have another encounter with Valerie, but now that Kade had verified what Sierra had said, Valerie needed to be interrogated. Jaycee would indeed want to hear what the woman had to say about her finances.

"Were the withdrawals enough to pay for the setup of the baby farms?" Josh asked.

"Could have been. Hard to say just how much an operation like that would need. The rent was very low on the ranch where Jaycee was held. Of course, the name of the lease turned out to be bogus."

Of course. "Is there anything in the lease agreement that could give us the person's real identity? Like a signature maybe, or an address?"

"Nothing. The agreement was done over the phone and the documents then faxed to the owner. The renter's name is Harold Wesson, and there was a fake credit check set up for him prior to the rental agreement. That's disappeared now."

Someone had covered their tracks. Still, the person in charge had hired a lot of people. Guards, nannies and even doctors. All of that couldn't be cheap. And the pay had to have been high enough to keep all these employees quiet. There's no way these people could have worked on a baby farm and not realized they were doing something illegal.

"The guards where I was held were thugs," Jaycee told him. "I'm betting they all had criminal records. There was nothing in the rubble to link back to one of them?"

"Nothing," Kade verified. "The explosion took care of that."

And that was no doubt the reason the explosive devices had been set. Heaven knows how long they'd been in place. Probably the entire time she'd been held captive. The guards had always threatened that things were rigged to explode, but she'd never seen any proof of it.

"What about the vehicles that were at the baby farm?" Josh asked. "I know they were destroyed in the blast, but were you able to get any of the vehicle identification numbers?"

"Just two, and the first led us back to this alias, Harold Wesson. The truck was a cash purchase, and the seller wasn't able to give us much of a description. The second one was a vehicle that'd been reported stolen six months ago."

Jaycee wanted to scream, but she was too tired to waste that kind of energy. It was just so frustrating that this snake hadn't left more evidence behind.

"What kind of gut feeling do you have about Bryson

and Valerie?" Kade asked. "Any chance they could have funded this together?"

"Yes," Josh and she said in unison.

"They're too chummy if you ask me," Josh continued. "And I don't trust them. Sierra included."

"Glad you agree, because I need search warrants on both Bryson and Valerie to do any further digging."

And that reminded Jaycee of something else that was on their to-do list. "What about the search warrant for Sierra's place?"

"We finally got a signature on it, and agents are on the way over there now to execute it. By the way, any sign of her?"

"None so far, but Grayson and a couple of others are out looking," Josh answered.

If Sierra was truly innocent in all of this, Jaycee hoped Grayson found her before those guards did.

"Gotta go," Josh told his cousin. "Let me know if anything turns up in the search at Sierra's place." He paused. "And I'll let you know if anything comes of the meeting I'm about to have with someone claiming to be an escapee from one of the baby farms."

Now it was Kade's turn to pause. "You need some backup?"

Jaycee released the breath she'd been holding. Kade could have just threatened to nix the meeting, claiming that this was a federal matter now. Technically, it was. But his offer was the opposite of nixing it.

"I wouldn't say no to backup," Josh answered.

"When and where's the meeting?" Kade asked.

Josh rattled off the details, his gaze coming back to her again. "This woman says if Jaycee doesn't show up, then neither will she."

Kade cursed. "I'm guessing you're more than a little hesitant about that, and Jaycee wants to do it?"

Boy, did he hit the nail on the head.

"Yeah," Josh finally said.

"Okay," Kade continued. "There's an agent in the area taking one last look at the baby farm that was blown up. I'll get him over to the cemetery right now to secure the perimeter, and I'll meet him there. If we see anything suspicious, you can get Jaycee out of there fast."

"Thanks." Josh ended the call and snapped toward her. "The way I see it, I've got three choices. With Grayson and the others tied up with finding Sierra, I could leave you here with Gage and Bree. Take you back to the ranch. Or Gage and Bree can come with us and guard you during the meeting."

"You know which option I want. And it's the only one that's going to get us answers from Miranda."

He stood there, jaw muscles stirring and his forehead bunched up. "I don't want to regret this," he said under his breath.

"Neither do I." She touched his arm, rubbed gently, hoping it would soothe him. "But I also don't want any other women held captive if I can do anything to stop it."

The muscles kept stirring, and she wondered if he was thinking about another rogue investigation. The one that'd nearly gotten him killed before she'd been taken captive.

She wanted to tell him that it wouldn't happen again, but any reassurance she could give him would only be wishful thinking on her part. Jaycee only knew this was something she had to do.

Without saying anything, Josh went to the front of the building. She couldn't hear what he told Gage, but it prompted Gage to make a call. Then Gage went back to talk to Bree.

"They're coming with us," Josh informed her. "Another deputy will be here soon to cover the office." He took her by the shoulders and met her eye to eye. "I only want Miranda to get a glimpse of you. You won't get out of the vehicle. And you won't take any unnecessary chances. Agreed?"

She nodded.

Josh still didn't jump to say she could go, but he surprised her when he leaned in, popped a kiss on her cheek.

"Take one of the guns," he instructed.

Jaycee did. A Glock and some extra ammo. She prayed they wouldn't need it, but they might not just run into Miranda at the cemetery. The guards could be there, too.

It didn't take long for another deputy to arrive, and Josh, Bree, Gage and she got into an SUV parked behind the sheriff's office. By her estimations, they weren't supposed to meet Miranda for at least another hour, but maybe the woman would arrive early so they could learn the truth, put Miranda in protective custody and get the heck out of there.

With Josh behind the wheel, they drove out of town. And all of them kept watch. She didn't see any signs of Valerie and Bryson. Nor the guards. She hoped it stayed that way.

The sun was blinding. Already too hot considering it was still spring, and despite the AC running, Jaycee felt the beads of sweat pop out on her forehead. Nerves, maybe. She wasn't having second thoughts about doing this, but she was afraid. Not just for her baby, but for everyone involved in this tangled mess.

Josh's phone rang, and without taking his eyes off the road, he pressed the answer button. A moment later, she heard Kade's voice.

"We're in place," Kade said. "I'm on the east side of the cemetery. Agent Seth Calder's on the west. I can see the road, and he's got a good view of the woods that aren't that far away."

"Any sign of a woman we're supposed to meet?" Josh asked.

"No sign of anyone right now, and I'm using thermal-imaging binoculars so I'll be able to see her or anyone else if they come from the woods. I'll let you know when or if she gets here."

"Thanks, we're about five minutes out." Josh ended the call and met her gaze in the mirror. "If she doesn't show soon, we're leaving. I don't want to sit out here in the open for too long."

Maybe Miranda would call. Because Jaycee didn't want to be sitting ducks, either.

Josh took a turn onto a rural road, then another, and she saw the cemetery just ahead.

"Mercy," Jaycee mumbled, "why the heck would Miranda pick this place?"

It wasn't the pristine church cemetery that Jaycee had expected. In fact, there was no church at all. No buildings. Just some bleached headstones on a weed-infested hill. There were a few large oaks dotting the area and thicker woods farther away, but even they looked dark and sinister. Like the setting for a horror movie.

No vehicles in sight. Of course, there were likely trails nearby where she could have hidden a car. Maybe Miranda had stolen a vehicle along with the phone she'd used to call them.

Or maybe this was all a ruse.

Josh didn't drive all the way up the hill. He pulled onto the narrow shoulder about thirty yards from the cemetery, and both Gage and he took out binoculars. Bree turned in the seat to keep a watch on the road behind them, so Jaycee took the right side. There were some trees in that area, too.

An ideal place for armed guards to hide.

But Jaycee was hoping Kade would be able to pinpoint anyone before the person got in a position to shoot at them.

"Nothing," Josh said several moments later, and Gage echoed an agreement.

Josh's phone rang, the sound knifing through the SUV and through her. "It's that woman again," the emergency dispatcher said, and he put Miranda's call through.

"They're after me," Miranda blurted out. Her words ran together, and she seemed out of breath. "Did you send them to kill me?"

"I didn't send anyone. But there are two FBI agents by the cemetery. They won't hurt you."

"These guys aren't agents, and they're definitely trying to kill me."

Oh, God. Miranda was in trouble. She thought of Valerie and Bryson outside the office door, listening to the conversation. Had one or both of them alerted the guards?

If so, they were no doubt connected to the baby farms.

"Who's after you and where are you?" Josh demanded.

"The guards. They're chasing me." And that's all Miranda said for several moments. "I'm near the cemetery, but the meeting is off. If I go out there now, they'll kill me."

The last word had no sooner left her mouth when the sound of a shot cracked through the air.

Chapter Twelve

Josh didn't have to tell Jaycee to get down. She was already headed that way before he glanced back at her. Like the rest of them, though, she kept her gun ready.

His phone rang again, and when Josh saw Kade's name on the screen, he answered it right away. "Do you see Miranda?" Josh asked.

"No. But I just picked up someone on the thermal scan. A person in the woods directly ahead of me. He or she appears to be running."

"You see just one person?" Josh pressed. "Because she says someone's chasing her."

"If they are, I'm not seeing them yet."

That didn't mean they weren't there. Josh knew there were ways to fool a thermal scan, including special clothing or simply hiding behind a pile of rocks that had been warmed by the sun. Still, Miranda had made it seem as if the guards were right on her heels.

Another shot.

It had come from the woods, but he couldn't pinpoint it beyond that.

"I need to go after her," Josh told the others. "I can't leave her out there to die."

"No." Jaycee took hold of his shoulder to stop him from opening the door.

"It's my job," he reminded her, and he eased her hand away. "I'll be back." He glanced at Gage and Bree. "Make sure Jaycee stays put."

But he figured she wouldn't go out there. Too risky for the baby. Josh knew it was risky for him, too, so he texted Kade for an update.

See the attackers? Josh asked, and he didn't have to wait long for an answer.

Whoever's out there, the person just went down to the ground. They're not moving.

Mercy. That meant Miranda could have been shot.

I'm going closer to check on her now, Kade texted a moment later.

I'll be coming in right behind you. And Josh started up the hill.

He soon caught sight of Kade and the other agent. They were moving toward the woods. Josh kept low. Kept his gun ready. And he followed them, cutting across the cemetery. Just ahead, a few yards into the woods, Kade stopped, stooped down and touched something while the other agent stood watch.

Hell. Had Kade found blood?

Josh hurried, running now, and he saw Kade take out his phone. "I'm calling an ambulance. She's alive."

Thank God.

But Josh did a double take when he saw the woman on the ground. Not Miranda.

But Sierra.

She was moaning and had a cut on her head, and blood was trickling down to her eyebrow. It didn't look serious, but a blow to the head was never good—especially since she was pregnant.

"What happened to you?" Josh asked, kneeling down beside her. He also continued to keep watch around them. "Why are you out here?"

"I was supposed to meet Miranda." Her words were barely a whisper and slurred. She moaned again. "She called and asked me to meet her here, but there were men with guns. Those guards," she added, and the tears rolled down her cheeks.

"There's no sign of them now," Josh told her.

But that didn't mean they weren't close by. He hoped it didn't take long for the ambulance to get there because he didn't want Sierra or Jaycee in the middle of another gunfight. And as long as those guards were in the area, a gunfight was likely.

Josh was about to ask Sierra why she'd run away from the hospital, but she lifted her hand. She had something clutched between her fingers.

A small piece of torn paper.

"Miranda was going to give me the address of the baby farm," Sierra continued. "And the person who's in charge. She tried to hand me the note, but then the guards came and we had to get away from them. I lost sight of her."

Using just the tips of his index and middle fingers, Josh eased the paper from her fingers. The ink was smeared, maybe from the perspiration on Sierra's hand, but he could just make out a name.

Valerie.

Oh, man.

Did she have something to do with this?

Josh wasn't sure how reliable Miranda was, but since Valerie was already a suspect and had those suspicious cash withdrawals from her bank accounts, this moved her to the top of his suspect list.

There was something else on the paper, but the writing was smeared and Josh couldn't read it. He needed to have it analyzed.

"We'll wait with her for the ambulance to arrive," Kade offered. "Why don't you go ahead, take the note and get Jaycee out of here?"

It was a generous offer, and Josh took him up on it. "Thanks. But keep an eye on her. The last time she was at the hospital, she ran."

Though he doubted Sierra would pull that stunt again. The head injury had clearly shaken her.

Josh went back to the SUV, where Jaycee, Gage and Bree had a dozen questions, but he didn't have many answers. "It was Sierra out there." He rummaged through the SUV and found an evidence bag for the piece of paper.

Bree and Gage just looked ready for more questions, but Jaycee leaned across the seat and hugged him when he got behind the wheel. It surprised him a little.

All right, it surprised him a lot.

Those walls he'd built between them were crumbling fast. No doubt because she was the mother of his child. And Josh was having a hard time figuring out how to stop it from being anything more.

That hug sure didn't help.

"Thank God you're all right," she whispered. "How's Sierra?"

"I think she'll be fine, but Kade called an ambulance." He started the engine and got them out of there in case the guards made a return appearance, and he passed his phone to Jaycee. "Scroll through the numbers and call Valerie."

Her eyes widened. "Why? You think she had something to do with this?"

"Maybe." And he waited until Jaycee had the woman on the line before he said anything else. "Who did you tell about the meeting with the woman who escaped?" Josh asked Valerie.

"I don't know what you mean. I didn't tell anyone."

"Well, someone did, and because of the snitch, your sister was attacked."

"Oh, my God. Is she all right?"

"No." That was stretching the truth, but he didn't want to give Valerie any reassurances. "When we found her, she was clutching a piece of a note that the escaped woman had given her. The note had your name on it. Care to tell me why?"

Valerie's gasp came through loud and clear, but whether it was genuine or not was anyone's guess. "I have no idea." She muttered something Josh didn't catch. "I handle adoptions sometimes, but I swear none of them have any connection to this black-market operation."

"Then why did you withdraw a small fortune right about the time this operation started up?" And he didn't bother to make that sound civil. By God, he wanted answers, and he wanted them now.

"Withdrawals?" Valerie repeated. "I took money out, yes, but not for anything illegal. My law partner had some huge medical bills that his insurance didn't cover, and I gave him a couple of loans, that's all."

"I want proof of that. Get down to the Silver Creek sheriff's office so I can take your statement, and bring copies of your bank records with you. While you're at it, I want proof of these loans. Medical records, statements, whatever you have that could possibly convince me you're not guilty."

"Of course I'll come. But I won't be treated like a criminal."

"You will be if you are one," Josh fired back. "Be there in one hour."

"Wait," Valerie said when Josh was about to hit the

end-call button. "What about my sister? Is Sierra on the way to the hospital?"

"Yeah. In an ambulance, and she'll have FBI escort. In other words, if Sierra says she doesn't want to see you, then you're not getting close to her." Josh punched the end-call button.

"You believe she's telling the truth about the withdrawals?" Gage asked.

But Josh just shook his head. It would be so much easier if Valerie was guilty. Then they could arrest her and maybe dangle a plea bargain in front of her so she'd give them details of the entire baby farm operation. But so far, everything had been circumstantial.

What they needed was proof.

Or a confession.

Now, that was something he could maybe make happen if he pressed Sierra hard enough. And he intended to press her *hard*.

Josh met Jaycee's gaze in the rearview mirror. The nerves were still there, right at the surface. And he silently cursed what this was doing to her. Too bad there wasn't much he could do about it. The danger just kept coming no matter how hard he tried to keep her safe.

He drove back to the sheriff's office, grabbed the evidence bag and hurried Jaycee inside. However, they hadn't even made it to his office before his phone rang. Hell. He couldn't deal with any more bad news right now, but it was his cousin Nate.

"You okay?" Nate asked the moment that Josh answered. "Just got off the phone with Kade and he told me what was going on."

"I've been better."

Jaycee took the evidence bag from him. Ready to examine that note again. So despite everything, she was clearly still an FBI agent looking for the truth.

"I just got a report back on the search at Sierra DeSilva's apartment," Nate continued. "The place had been trashed, and I'm pretty sure a lot of stuff was removed before we got there. Including her computer and the copies of those bank records that were supposedly there."

Great.

"There's more," Nate went on. "I'm sending you a photo of it now."

Judging from Nate's tone, this wouldn't be good, either, so Josh tried to brace himself. The photo loaded slowly, but pretty soon he saw the words that'd been scrawled on what appeared to be her bedroom wall.

Talk and you die.

"It was written with her lipstick," Nate explained. "I'll have the place processed for fibers, prints—anything—and I'll call if we find anything else."

Josh mumbled a thanks, ended the call and took a deep breath. Jaycee was right there, and pulled a bottle of water from the fridge. She opened it, had a sip and then passed it to him. It wasn't a shot of whiskey, but it'd have to do.

"Today, I really hated the job," Jaycee said. "I didn't like you going out there after those shots had been fired."

He lifted his shoulder, had some more water. "You hugged me."

"Yes." She dodged his gaze. "Sorry about that. It was another 'getting caught up in the moment' reaction."

So that was all there was to it. Relief that he hadn't been shot or killed. Funny, it'd felt like more. Good thing it wasn't.

At least he thought it was a good thing.

Josh had a dozen things to do before Valerie showed, but he wanted to take just a minute to test his "good thing

it wasn't" theory. He reached out, put his hand around the
back of Jaycee's neck and eased her to him.

He kissed her.

Jaycee made a little sound of surprise but didn't pull
away. She kissed him right back.

The taste of her slammed through him, and his senses
went into overdrive. The feel of her in his arms. Her breasts
against his chest. The sound of surprise that melted into
one of pleasure.

He pulled back. Wasn't easy. But he forced himself to
do it so he could assess things. Now, that was easy. He'd
made another mistake, because using a kiss to test a theory was playing with a giant ball of fire.

"Sorry," he murmured.

"You're sure about being sorry?" No gaze dodging this
time. She was staring at him.

No, he wasn't, and that was what made him truly sorry.
Or maybe just stupid. "This has to stop. Agreed?" he
asked, but there would be only one right answer.

And Jaycee gave it to him. She nodded. However, she
stared at him a moment as if trying to figure out if stopping was something they could genuinely do.

Maybe they couldn't.

"Pretend if you have to," he added.

Another nod. "I can pretend."

Not exactly the hands-off declaration they should be
making, but it would do for now.

Cursing under his breath, Josh forced his mind back
where it should be—on work. He put on a pair of plastic
gloves and took the torn note from the evidence bag so
he could have a better look. Soon, he'd need to send it to
the lab, but first he wanted to see if he could make out the
rest of what it said.

"That's definitely Valerie's name," Jaycee said, pointing to the top line. Her finger accidentally brushed against his arm, and she backed away.

Far away.

Obviously, she had this pretense thing down pat. Well, except for the slight throat clearing she made. And the glance she gave him. Josh ignored both. He ignored everything except the evidence in front of him.

"Of course, she might say it refers to another Valerie," he added.

If so, it wouldn't do her any good. Because she was tied to this case through her sister. What he needed, though, was more than just something to tie her to the case. He needed proof that she was guilty. Josh studied the lines below Valerie's name.

"I think it says William," Jaycee said. Without touching the paper or him, she scrolled her finger above the word below Valerie's name, tracing the scrawled letters.

Josh nodded. He could see it. But who the heck was William? That name hadn't come up in the investigation.

Yet.

He turned the paper at a slightly different angle and put his attention on the next two words. The last one was four letters, all lowercase.

"Road?" Josh mumbled. He tried other possibilities, but that was the only one he could think of that worked. And that led him to the middle word.

"William Casey Road," he said. "It's about ten miles outside of town."

He hurried to his computer so he could access land records. It took him several moments to work through the passwords and get to the right page. Thankfully, there weren't a lot of people living on William Casey Road because it was mainly ranch and farmland. And one name in particular snagged his attention.

Bingo.

"Last year Bryson bought an abandoned ranch on William Casey Road."

"If you ask me, Bryson doesn't look like the ranching type."

No. He didn't. And even though a lot of people were buying ranch land as an investment because of its rock-bottom prices, Bryson could be using it for something else.

Like a baby farm.

He took out his phone and called Grayson. Thankfully his cousin answered on the first ring. "We might have a lead. Bryson owns a ranch at 623 William Casey Road. Can you get someone out there right away to check on the place?"

"Dade and I'll go. Mason and Kade can stay at the hospital with Sierra."

"How's she doing?" And Josh hated that he hadn't already checked on her.

"She's with the doctor now. And don't worry. We'll cover all exits just in case she decides to jackrabbit again."

Good. Because he needed to interrogate Sierra again, too.

"I'll let you know if we find anything at Bryson's place," Grayson assured him, and ended the call.

"Speaking of Bryson, where do you think he is?" Jaycee asked.

He hoped the man was at the baby farm so Grayson could arrest him on the spot and close the place down. Josh didn't intend to give Bryson a heads-up about Grayson's visit, but he did want to check on the man to see what he had to say about this latest attack on Sierra. Josh was betting that Valerie had already contacted him and spilled everything she'd learned.

Josh punched in Bryson's number. Waited. It rang so long that Josh was about to hang up, but he finally answered.

Except it wasn't Bryson.

"Deputy Ryland," a woman answered. She sounded frantic. "I'm Bryson's secretary. He left in a hurry and didn't take his phone. Oh, God. Please tell me you can stop him."

Josh pulled back his shoulders. "Stop him? Why would I need to stop him?"

"Because he intends to hurt her. He was so angry. I've never seen him like that before. He drove out of here like a crazy man."

"Slow down," Josh insisted. "Where was Bryson going?"

"To the Silver Creek hospital. He heard that Sierra would be there. Please, Deputy Ryland, go after him. Because as angry as Bryson is, I'm afraid he'll kill her."

Chapter Thirteen

Jaycee could hear the shouts when they stepped into the emergency room of the Silver Creek hospital. And there was no mistaking that the person doing the shouting was none other than Bryson.

Josh and she followed the noise and found him outside one of the E.R. examining rooms. He was demanding to go inside, but Mason had blocked his way. Considering that Mason looked like an ornery vampire who was about to rip off Bryson's head, Jaycee was surprised the man was continuing his tirade.

"I will see her!" Bryson shouted. "Sierra, get out here now!"

That was apparently all Mason intended to put up with because he caught on to Bryson's shoulder and slammed the man face-first against the wall. Bryson sputtered out a cough but seemed too stunned to do anything but cooperate. Mason cuffed him and then spun him back around.

"You yell one more time," Mason warned him, his voice dark and dangerous, "and I *will* make you hush."

Finally, Bryson shut up, but the moment he spotted Josh and her approaching, he apparently decided to plead his case to them.

"Sierra's in there, and I have to talk to her now." Bryson

kept his voice at a normal level, probably because Mason was still in his face.

"Sierra's been through an ordeal," Jaycee reminded him. "I think she needs to see the doctor more than she needs to talk to you."

Bryson snarled something she didn't catch, and he turned back to Mason. "Take off the cuffs."

Mason didn't jump to answer that. "You planning to do more yelling?"

"No," Bryson said through clenched teeth.

Mason kept staring at the man, and his stare was a lot worse than Bryson's glare. "What about it, Josh?" Mason asked without looking at his cousin. "You want the cuffs on or off when you talk to this loudmouthed dirt wad?"

Josh eyed Bryson for several seconds. "Off for now, but if he raises his voice again or tries to go in that room with Sierra, then I'll cuff and arrest him."

Clearly, that didn't please Bryson, but he kept his mouth shut when Mason took off the cuffs. Mason shot Bryson another warning glare, then sank down in one of the waiting room chairs and stretched out his legs.

"You know what Sierra did?" Bryson asked them, but he didn't wait for an answer. "She tried to blackmail me again. She sent me a letter this time, demanding a half million dollars for my own baby."

A letter? Now, that was a surprise. Jaycee couldn't figure out when the woman had had time to do that, considering she'd been on the run.

Josh walked closer, positioning himself between Bryson and the examining room door. "Did you know that someone clubbed her on her forehead?"

"No." Bryson's breath caught as if he was genuinely surprised, and if he was acting, it was good. "I thought she was faking an injury so she wouldn't have to deal with me."

Well, Jaycee couldn't rule that out. "It seems odd, though, that she'd make a demand for all that money and then try to dodge you."

"She knew I'd be furious."

"Yeah," Josh agreed. "But getting clubbed on the head isn't my first choice of ways to avoid a man's fury."

Bryson opened his mouth, closed it and then cursed. "How badly is she hurt?"

"We're not sure," Josh answered. "In fact, we're not sure of a lot of things right now. We were supposed to meet another woman in an area just outside of town, and Sierra showed up instead."

What Josh didn't mention was the note and the ranch property that was hopefully being checked out as they spoke. While she was hoping, Jaycee added that Grayson and his brother would find enough evidence for them to make an arrest in connection with the baby farms. It didn't matter if it was Bryson, Valerie or even Sierra, Jaycee just wanted this person off the streets and behind bars.

"Any idea why Sierra was at that meeting?" Josh asked.

Bryson immediately shook his head. "None. The only thing I know about Sierra is that she's up to her old tricks. But I won't be blackmailed. If I had that kind of money, I wouldn't be paying it to her."

"But what about your *heir?*" Jaycee purposely used that term instead of baby.

"I'll challenge her for custody. I already have the test to establish paternity, and it shouldn't be hard to prove her an unfit mother."

That was the pot calling the kettle black, because in her opinion Bryson was an unfit father.

Unlike Josh.

Jaycee hated that the thought popped into her head, but she couldn't shut it out. Josh was a good man, but it was also clear that he had a huge interest in this baby she was carrying. Maybe Josh would pull a Bryson and challenge her for custody, too.

If he did, he could win.

She didn't have family support like Josh did, and she was the daughter of not one but two convicted felons. Her time in foster care wouldn't help, either, because she'd been pretty much labeled a juvenile delinquent. Hardly a good track record for a mother fighting for custody of her child.

"What's the matter?" she heard Josh ask.

It took her a moment to realize he was looking at her because she'd made a soft moaning sound at the prospect of losing her child to him.

"Nothing," she mumbled and tried to get her mind back on Bryson. But Josh obviously didn't believe her, because he took her by the shoulders and had her lean against the wall. He studied her eyes.

"Come on," Josh insisted. "I'll take you to the cafeteria and get you something to eat."

She wasn't hungry. Hard to be hungry with the threat of those armed guards looming over them, but Jaycee figured it would do the baby some good if she ate something. Her mealtimes had been regimented when she was being held at the baby farm, but her life had been so chaotic since Josh had rescued her.

"What about Valerie?" she asked. "Shouldn't we get back to the sheriff's office?"

"Gage can handle the interview," Josh insisted. "While we're here, I want you to get checked out by a doctor. Just to make sure everything's okay." A muscle flickered in his jaw. "There's no telling what those guards did to you."

Jaycee was certain they hadn't done anything to harm the baby—especially since a healthy baby had been all they'd wanted. Still, an exam wouldn't hurt.

Josh looked back at Mason and motioned for him to watch Bryson again, and he led her down a corridor. He'd only made it a few steps when he got a text.

"Not more bad news?" she asked when he looked at the screen.

He shook his head but then lifted his shoulder. "The text was from Melissa Garza, the woman who's marrying my uncle this weekend. She wanted us to know that the decorators are at the ranch now."

That could be bad. *Very* bad. "These people were screened for security?"

"Sure, but it's a big crew, so it's possible for someone to slip through." He glanced at her, probably trying to reassure her with that look. "Everyone's being checked for weapons, and when we get back, I'll make sure to turn on the security system in the apartment."

Jaycee tried not to overreact to something as simple as arming a security system. Hard not to do, though, because Josh was right. It was possible for those guards to make it onto the ranch, and if they couldn't stop them, she at least wanted to be alerted if one of them tried to break in while Josh and she were sleeping.

The cafeteria wasn't far, just a few doors away, and Jaycee got a sandwich and some milk. Josh got a chili dog, loaded, and some soggy-looking fries. He didn't waste any time before he started wolfing it down.

"Now, will you tell me what's wrong?" he asked.

Apparently, she no longer had the poker face that'd made her a decent undercover agent.

"The baby. Our baby," she clarified. "And custody. I know you said you only wanted to be part of the baby's life, but I'm worried that maybe you would change your mind when you gave it some more thought."

He stopped in midbite, staring at her from over the top

of that dripping chili dog. "Are you planning to challenge me to get full custody?"

She nearly choked on the sandwich. "No. But I figured you'd challenge me."

He dragged a fry through the chili, popped it in his mouth. "Right. Because I'm such good father material."

"But you are." He knew that.

Right?

Obviously not, judging from the flat look he gave her.

"I'm a mess," he continued, sounding disgusted with himself. "And let's not forget that my own mother left when I was a kid. Bad divorce," he added in a mumble. "My father was, well, absent after that despite being around. Grayson's the closest thing I ever had to a dad."

Jaycee was glad she had the sandwich because it gave her something to do. She nibbled on it while she tried to process what Josh had just told her. "I didn't know."

"Well, yeah, I don't share that with a lot of people." He paused, ate another fry. "Will you use that against me when you try to get full custody?"

"No." And she stretched that out a few syllables. "Remember, my parents did hard time for aggravated armed robbery and an assortment of other felonies. Plenty of people would argue that their criminal history makes me an unsuitable parent."

Great. Now she was handing him ammunition to use against her. Not that any of it had been a surprise, but it probably wasn't a good idea to remind him of it now. She didn't have time to talk her way out of the hole she'd just dug because Josh's phone rang.

"It's Mason," he let her know right before he answered it. He didn't put the call on speaker, probably because other diners were close by, and Jaycee couldn't hear what Mason said even when she leaned across the table.

"Sierra's water broke," Josh told her when he finished the call. "Her contractions are coming nonstop, and the doctor doesn't think it'll be long before she has the baby. They just moved her to Labor and Delivery, so Mason's heading over there, too, to make sure Bryson stays away."

That was good, but the timing of the labor perhaps wasn't so good. "Maybe the trauma of what happened in the woods caused her contractions to start."

But Josh just shrugged. "Mason had a quick word with the doctor. He said the cut on Sierra's head was superficial, hardly more than a scratch. It didn't even need stitches."

Jaycee didn't have to give that much thought. "You think she did it herself?"

Another shrug, and he continued to eat. "I think Sierra's capable of just about anything. And while I don't like the idea of Bryson trying to confront her at a time like this, I'd be pissed, too, if she tried to blackmail me like that."

Jaycee silently agreed, and she cringed at the thought of Bryson raising the child. Maybe just having an heir would be enough for him to collect the rest of his inheritance, and that way he wouldn't need to have an active part in his son's or daughter's life. Of course, Sierra wouldn't exactly qualify for mother of the year, either.

Josh finished his fries and hot dog and took out his phone again. "I'm calling Grayson to see if he made it out to Bryson's property. After that, I need to find out how the interrogation is going with Valerie, and then I can see about getting you examined. Then I can take you to the ranch so you can have a nap."

The married-to-the-badge part of her wanted to insist that they stay at the sheriff's office to deal with anything else that might come up. But she was exhausted. In need of a nap.

And craving doughnuts.

She looked back at the display cases, but didn't see any in the cafeteria. "You think there's a place nearby where I can get a doughnut?"

"We can hit the drive-through on the way home," Josh murmured right before Grayson came on the line. Again, she couldn't hear what he was saying, but it caused Josh's forehead to bunch up.

Please, no more bad news. Jaycee had already had her fill of that today. Besides, she really was tired. At the baby farm, she'd slept most of the day. When she wasn't figuring out how to escape. But since Josh had rescued her, there hadn't been time in between attacks for her to get much rest.

"They didn't find anything at the ranch," Josh said after he ended the call. He stood. "No sign that anyone had been there recently, but they'll keep looking."

It would have been nice to find something incriminating, but maybe there was still a chance for that. "What if it's to be a future site for a baby farm?"

Josh nodded. "Grayson's putting up a hidden surveillance camera on the porch of the abandoned house. It's motion activated, so if anyone goes out there, we'll know about it."

And she wouldn't be surprised to see Valerie, Bryson or those missing guards making that visit. Or even Sierra once she'd had her baby and then recovered. That meant they might have to wait awhile for any possible answers they might get there.

As they turned toward the exit, Jaycee saw a woman making a beeline for them. She was tall and rail thin, and had choppy blond hair. Even though the woman wasn't armed and didn't appear to be a threat, Josh still stepped between her and Jaycee.

"Deputy Josh Ryland," the woman said, extending her hand for him to shake.

"Who are you?" Josh snapped. He darn sure didn't shake her hand.

"I'm Miranda Culley. And I understand you and Agent Finney have been looking for me."

Chapter Fourteen

Josh just stared at their visitor. He didn't recognize her, but he sure as heck recognized her name. His gaze dropped to the woman's stomach.

Flat.

Definitely not pregnant.

And that wasn't the only thing that snagged his attention. Miranda was wearing what appeared to be a waitress uniform. She definitely didn't look like someone who'd just escaped armed guards and a baby farm.

"Did you recently have a baby?" Josh asked.

"No." She didn't exactly seem comfortable with the question, and she cleared her throat. "I've never been pregnant. Nor have I actually been missing."

"But no one at your job knew where you were," Jaycee pointed out.

"Because I was having some trouble with my boss hitting on me. I didn't leave because I was pregnant. I left because I wanted to get away from him. So I certainly wasn't going to tell him where I was going."

Josh shook his head. "What about the calls you made to me through the emergency dispatcher?"

"I didn't make the calls, either." Miranda paused, swallowed hard. "Look, I'm not sure what's going on, Deputy Ryland, but a friend from the diner where I used to work emailed me and told me you were trying to find me because of those calls. That's when I realized someone must have been impersonating me. My name's not that common. I don't think there's another Miranda Culley in the state."

He searched her eyes and body language for any sign she was lying, but he saw nothing other than a confused, frightened woman. Still, he took out his phone and pressed the record function.

"I need a sample of your voice," Josh explained. "So it can be compared to the 911 recordings."

She didn't refuse. In fact, she moved closer to the phone. "Am I in danger?" Miranda asked.

Josh couldn't swear to her that she wasn't, because he didn't know what was going on either. "Has anyone been following you? Had any hang-up calls?"

She shook her head to both. "Not that I know of."

"Someone could have just used your name," he explained. He kept the recorder on, hoping to get a decent sample of her voice along with some answers. "Maybe because the person knew we'd check and find that missing persons report your boss filed on you."

And it wouldn't have been hard to find such a report, since they were often posted on the internet.

"Do you have any idea who would have done something like impersonate you?" Josh pressed.

"None. Like I said, I was having trouble with my boss, but I don't think he'd do this just to find me. Would he?"

Probably not, since it would mean he would have gotten access to information about the baby farm and then involved himself in a high-profile investigation. Pretty risky when it would have been easier just to try to worm the info from someone who knew Miranda.

"You have any friends you can stay with until this is over?" he asked.

"Yes. My boyfriend."

"Then go to him and call me at the Silver Creek sheriff's office if anyone suspicious contacts you." Josh turned off the recorder.

The woman gave a shaky nod, thanked him and hurried out. Josh watched her leave and wanted to curse. He'd thought Miranda would be a solid lead, someone who could give him information about the owner of the baby farms, but she seemed to be just another dead end.

"Why would someone have impersonated her?" Jaycee questioned.

Josh had been asking himself the same thing, and he had a theory. One that Jaycee wasn't going to like. "To draw us out into the open. If one of our suspects had asked for a meeting, we might have said no. But it's hard to say no to a woman who's running for her life and claiming we're the only people she can trust."

Jaycee made a sound to indicate she was thinking about that, and then she groaned softly. "But something must have gone wrong at the cemetery. Maybe because the FBI agents showed up. Or maybe because Sierra did."

Either was possible, but Josh had a way of checking who'd set up that meeting. Well, maybe. He took out his phone to make another call. In case someone was following Miranda, it probably wasn't a good idea for Jaycee and him to hang around the hospital. Her checkup would have to wait a little while longer.

"Sawyer," he said when his brother came on the line. "I need some 911 tapes analyzed."

Josh gave Sawyer the date and approximate times of the possible imposter's calls and sent him the recording of Miranda's voice. If the woman wasn't lying about having made those calls—and Josh didn't think she was—then maybe they'd soon know who did make them.

Josh finished talking with Sawyer and made another call—to Gage at the sheriff's office. He asked his cousin to come to the hospital so he'd have some backup and extra security when he left with Jaycee. Gage assured him that he was on the way, and it wouldn't take him long to get there since the sheriff's office was just up the street.

However, Jaycee and he had just made it out of the cafeteria when his phone rang again, and this time it was Mason's name on the screen.

"Sierra had the baby," Mason said. "A girl. According to the doc, both of them are healthy."

That was good news, but that *good* wasn't coming through in Mason's voice. "Anything wrong?"

"Yeah. Sierra's already insisting she wants to leave the hospital, that she doesn't feel safe here. You got grounds to arrest her, because that might be the only way I get her to stay put?"

"No grounds." Josh huffed. Though he wished he did have reason to arrest her—or anybody else. "But I'm sure the doctor's not going to let her go."

"You'd think, but the way Sierra's driving everybody crazy with her fussing and carrying on, the doc might call her a taxi. You're sure she could be in danger?"

"No," Josh had to admit. "I'm not sure of much of anything right now."

"Then, hell, I might call her a taxi," Mason growled, and ended the call.

Josh was pretty sure his cousin was joking about that last part, but with Mason, you never knew.

"Should we go see Sierra?" Jaycee asked. "And try to talk her into staying put?"

"No. I doubt we can talk her into anything. Since she's not a witness, we can't force her to accept police protection. Besides, she might just want to get away from Bryson."

After all, the man had accused Sierra of trying to blackmail him. And maybe she had. Maybe she was ready to cut her losses and run. Or she could just want to get out of there before they found the proof to make that arrest.

Josh led Jaycee through the corridors, back through the emergency room and to the exit. The doors were glass, so he could see the parking lot, and he took a moment to look around, to make sure there weren't any suspicious people or vehicles out there. No one was milling around. But there were about a dozen vehicles parked in the same area as Josh.

He spotted Gage.

His cousin was sitting in his own truck, parked next to Josh. Gage stepped from his vehicle, had a look around, as well. "Don't see anyone," he called out to Josh.

"Move fast," Josh instructed Jaycee, and he led her out the doors and toward his truck. Before he could get her inside, Josh heard a sound he damn sure didn't want to hear.

Someone fired a shot.

JAYCEE PRAYED THAT the noise was a car backfiring.

No such luck.

A bullet blasted through the air and into the front of Josh's truck. At the same time, the fear and adrenaline slammed into her. And Josh shoved her forward to the side of the nearest vehicle, and then pushed her to the ground.

He drew his weapon and got ready to fire.

But there wasn't another shot.

"Stay inside!" Josh shouted to a woman who was about to come out through the exit doors. Thankfully, the woman did and ran back into the hospital.

With his gaze firing all around, Josh lifted his head a little. Jaycee couldn't see a thing because Josh was literally right in front of her, and the only thing she could hear was the May breeze and her pulse hammering.

"See anything?" Gage called out. She hoped he'd taken cover, as well.

"Nothing," Josh answered.

But just as he spoke, another shot came, smashing into the ground directly in front of them. Josh pushed her back and took aim.

"He's on the roof," Josh shouted to Gage.

Oh, mercy. Definitely not a good spot, since the shooter would be able to see them while having good cover from any shots coming his way. Besides, Josh and Gage couldn't just start randomly firing because someone inside the hospital could be hurt.

"Move back," Josh instructed.

He stayed in front of her as Jaycee scrambled to get behind the rear of the car. It meant the shooter likely wouldn't be able to see her, but he would certainly be able to see Josh.

The next bullet proved that.

It came straight toward Josh, tearing across the concrete and scattering debris right at them. Jaycee caught on to his arm, pulled him back with her.

Gage returned fire. A single shot. But Jaycee couldn't tell where it went.

"It's me. Don't shoot," she heard Gage say a split second before he dived behind the car with them. "He's behind the big AC unit on the left. I got just a glimpse of him when he came out to fire."

Jaycee hadn't gotten a glimpse, but she was betting this was one of the armed guards who'd escaped. "Is he alone?"

Gage shook his head. "Not sure. I only saw one, but there could be others. Plenty of places to hide up there."

Yes, and any other backup that came to assist them

could be walking right into an ambush. Of course, the same could be said for anyone who was coming in to assist the shooter. Gage and Josh would see anyone trying to cut through the parking lot. On this side anyway.

"Anyone have a gun I can use?" Jaycee asked.

Josh took his from his boot holster but then shot her a warning glare. "That doesn't mean I want you up and shooting. Stay down."

She would. For the baby's sake. But she wanted the gun just in case this went from bad to worse. She figured Josh and Gage would do everything within their power to protect her, but if something happened and they got separated, then she wanted to be able to fight back.

Gage's phone buzzed, just a split second before there was another shot.

"It's Mason," Gage relayed and then answered the call. "He's on the roof. Make sure no one leaves the hospital. Tell Grayson to keep his distance, too. But try to get someone on the back side of that roof so you can stop this fool." He hung up and shoved the phone back into his pocket.

"This guy's being careful about his shots," Josh mumbled.

Yes, he was. Single shots that'd come darn close to Josh, but if the guy was heavily armed—and Jaycee figured he was—then he could be firing nonstop into the car until he ripped it to pieces.

And killed them.

But he wasn't doing that.

Why?

Only one answer came to mind. Because this wasn't a murder attempt, but rather a kidnapping. And that linked it right back to the baby farm.

Jaycee turned to check behind her. She was on the ground, but she could see beneath some of the other vehi-

cles, and she saw something she definitely hadn't wanted
to see.

"Someone's crouched behind that dark green truck," she
whispered. She had to repeat it, though, because the guy
on the roof fired at them again, and Josh didn't hear her.

Josh whirled around, lowered himself to the concrete,
looked around. And cursed. "It could be someone just trying to get out of the path of those bullets."

However, he didn't sound very convinced of that. Neither was Jaycee. Especially when the person moved and
darted behind another vehicle. One that was closer to Josh,
Gage and her.

He was moving in for the kill. Well, the kill for Gage
and Josh. She was betting the guy would try to eliminate
them so he'd have less of a fight taking her.

But he was wrong about that.

Jaycee wouldn't give up without a hard fight, because
her baby's life depended on it.

"Watch the guy on the roof," Josh told Gage, and he
went even lower to the ground until he was practically on
his belly. He took aim.

Fired.

Judging from the sound, the bullet zinged off some
metal, but she couldn't tell what it hit. Definitely not the
person lurking there, because he returned fire almost immediately.

And so did the guy on the roof.

Cursing, Josh crawled over her, protecting her and the
baby with his body, and he fired at the shooter behind
them. Gage took a shot at the one of the roof.

Both gunmen fired back.

And that meant Josh, Gage and she were caught in the
middle.

This was exactly what Josh had no doubt wanted to

avoid, but here they were in a bad situation where he was having to put his life on the line to keep her safe.

The shots kept coming at them, pelting the ground and slamming into the vehicles. Jaycee wanted to fight back. To stop this. But she couldn't risk getting up. Because if these goons managed to kidnap her, they'd kill Josh and Gage.

Probably kill her, too, once they had what they wanted from her.

Jaycee wasn't sure exactly what they did indeed want, but if it was the baby, they weren't going to get it.

The shooters kept firing. Gage and Josh fired, too, but not as much. No doubt trying to conserve ammunition.

Gage's phone buzzed again, and without taking his attention from the guy on the roof, he took out his phone and slid it her way. She saw Grayson's name on the screen and answered it.

"We're pinned down," she let him know.

"Stay put. Tell Josh and Gage to get down, too. Mason's got everyone behind cover inside the hospital, and Dade, Bree and I are coming in."

"Grayson says for us all to get down," she relayed.

Josh and Gage both dropped down. Gage on the ground next to her, and Josh still on top of her.

They didn't have to wait long before Jaycee heard another shot. It hadn't come from the roof or behind them. This one had been fired to their right. And the shots didn't stop. They just kept shooting until she saw the man behind the car scramble to get away.

"He's on the run!" she heard Grayson shout. Jaycee also heard the sound of running footsteps. Not just one set but several.

There was another shot from the roof. Just one. She waited, holding her breath and praying that none of Josh's family had been hit. But if it'd happened, Grayson had been spared. He hurried toward them.

"Stay where you are," Grayson warned them. "Dade and I are going after the guy on the roof. Bree's blocking the back exit now in case he tries to get out that way."

This time Josh didn't listen.

"Watch Jaycee," he told Gage. "I'm going after the other gunman."

Chapter Fifteen

The shooters had gotten away.

That thought kept going through Josh's head like a broken record, and it didn't play any better than the first time he'd heard it.

He wasn't sure how that had happened, not with Gage and the others helping. But somehow the guys had managed to give them the slip, which meant they were still there.

Ready for another attack.

This one had been well planned, and obviously the two shooters had worked out solid escape routes before the attack had even started. Josh figured the one on the roof had gone through a ventilation duct to get inside the hospital, where he'd just blended in until he could walk out. It didn't help that neither Gage, Jaycee nor he could give accurate descriptions of the guys.

The other one Josh had been after had likely had a vehicle parked nearby. Again, he'd blended in with the rest of the traffic on Main Street.

Too bad the escape plans had worked.

But why had they tried to kidnap Jaycee again?

And there was no doubt in his mind that this had been a kidnapping attempt. The guy on the roof was supposed to take Josh out. Gage, too. Leaving the one in the parking lot to kidnap Jaycee. Obviously, they wanted her bad, or else they wouldn't have staged an attack in broad daylight.

Was it the baby they wanted?

Or was it Jaycee so they could eliminate her in case she'd seen something at the baby farm that she could use to make an arrest?

Josh didn't have answers for that and probably wouldn't until he managed to catch one of those guards and question him. And he would catch one. Too bad that might not happen before there was another attack.

That went through his head like a broken record, too.

At least he'd managed to get the doctor out to the ranch to examine Jaycee. From what the doc had been able to tell, everything was fine with both the baby and her. Josh needed to make sure things stayed that way.

He lay on the bed, stared up at the ceiling and listened to the sound of the shower running. Jaycee had been in there for a long time, but then she no doubt had a lot of tense muscles that needed relaxing. He wished he could say it was the end of the tension-causing events, but he couldn't.

This was just getting started.

He'd already verified that the woman who'd come to the hospital cafeteria was indeed Miranda Culley, and that she'd never been held captive at a baby farm and had not made those 911 calls to set up the meeting at the cemetery. So why had someone impersonated her?

To lure him out when he tried to rescue her?

Maybe.

But the lure hadn't worked because no one pretending to be Miranda had shown up. Still, Jaycee and he had gone out to that cemetery, and he might have been shot if he hadn't had plenty of backup with him. Jaycee could have been hurt, too, with a botched kidnapping.

Heck, they'd come close to being shot again today.

Josh touched the scar on his chest. It wasn't hurting much tonight. Probably because he'd had plenty of other things to occupy his mind.

Like keeping Jaycee safe.

He had to do a better job of that, but all the measures seemed temporary at this point. Especially now with the decorating crew for the wedding on the grounds.

Soon the caterers would arrive, too, and then the day after tomorrow, the guests. It was one wedding that Josh couldn't attend. No way. Not with several hundred guests expected, and he couldn't very well ask his uncle Boone to postpone it. That was why Josh had already called his brother about making arrangements for a safe house.

If he couldn't catch those armed guards and shut down the baby farms, then Jaycee and he would be joined at the hip, well, forever. A safe house and this apartment were going to get pretty darn small if things weren't settled soon.

His phone rang, something it'd been doing a lot since they'd arrived back at the ranch. Just calls to let him know that all their attempts to find those guards had failed. This time, he saw Grayson's name on the screen.

"Thought you'd like to know that Sierra left the hospital with her baby about an hour ago," Grayson said. "Mason tried to stop her. The doctor, too, but she wouldn't stay."

And that made her stupid. "Does she know about the latest shooting?"

"She knows. Still didn't change her mind. Before she left, Bryson made a fuss about seeing the baby," Grayson went on. "I finally had a nurse let him see her through the nursery window. He took one look at the baby, cursed a blue streak and said she wasn't his, that she didn't look like him. He stormed off, mumbling something about demanding another paternity test."

"Valerie did say that Sierra could have had the results of the first test faked." Of course, Valerie could have said that to shift suspicion from herself onto her.

"She repeated that to Bryson. Valerie was with him when he saw the baby."

Another case of being joined at the hip. That closeness between two of their suspects bothered Josh, but he wasn't sure what to make of it. Maybe it was something as simple as Valerie being his attorney. After the shooting today, however, he wasn't about to take anything at face value.

"What did Sierra have to say about Bryson and her sister's reactions?" Josh asked.

"Not much. She insists the child is Bryson's and says to prove it she'll have as many tests as he wants."

That didn't sound like the offer of a guilty woman. Unless Sierra figured she could fake those results, too. Of course, it could have been all talk, because Sierra had left the hospital for some reason. Maybe because she was afraid for her life or maybe just because she was afraid of what Bryson might do to her if he found out she was lying about the baby's paternity.

The bathroom door opened, and Jaycee stepped out. She was wearing a stark-white loaner bathrobe, and her face was flushed, no doubt from the warm steamy water. For just a split second Josh got an image of her standing in the shower.

Naked.

His imagination was a little too good in that area, because he felt the heat coil through his entire body. Of course, it didn't help that he had the real thing standing right in front of him and looking far better than a scared pregnant woman should look.

"Call me if anything comes up," he said to Grayson

when he managed to stop himself from being tongue-tied. He ended the call and sat up.

"No, you should stay there." Jaycee motioned for him to remain on the bed. "I'd imagine your back is sore from sleeping on the floor."

Well, it didn't feel good, but because of that heat coursing through him, it was best if he didn't stay on the bed. At the moment it wasn't a safe place to be. Because there was one stupid part of his body that might try to talk Jaycee into joining him there.

"Sierra left the hospital." He got off the bed, the mattress creaking a little. Stood. Faced her. "She took the baby with her."

Jaycee blew out a long breath. "I feel sorry for that child. Especially if Bryson is the father. The idea of him getting custody makes me a little ill."

Even though this was a serious discussion, she glanced at him. Then at the bed. She fidgeted with the tie on the terry-cloth robe, though it didn't look as if it needed any kind of adjustment.

Well, except for that V opening that went practically to her breasts.

The garment wasn't meant to be provocative, but it was on Jaycee. Her breasts looked ready to spill right out of there, and sadly, that stupid part of his body was hoping they did.

Just to give his head and his mouth something else to do, he tipped his head to the kitchen area. "Bessie, the cook, sent us over some beef stew with one of the ranch hands. It's in the microwave."

The stew didn't get much of a reaction, but her eyes widened when her attention went to the table and the plate of doughnuts covered with plastic wrap.

"I told Bessie about your doughnut craving," Josh explained, "and she fixed those for you, too. She said I'm to tell you though that they're not as good as the ones you'd get from the café in town."

The place they'd intended to stop before someone had tried to kill them.

That had certainly put a hold on the doughnut plans. Instead, Josh had rushed Jaycee back to the ranch, literally locked them inside and set the security system.

Jaycee gave a sheepish smile. "I'll have just one and then some stew." She crossed the room and dived into the plate of doughnuts.

"I swear, I ate healthy while I was a captive." She made that sound of pleasure again after she'd had a bite.

The sound that reminded Josh of sex, the bed and other things that he shouldn't be reminded of right now. Man, he really needed to get a grip.

But that didn't happen.

His eyes went wandering, and when Jaycee lifted the doughnut to take another bite, her robe shifted, and he got a glimpse of her breasts.

No bra.

No gown.

Unless she had on panties, she was butt naked beneath the robe. His body didn't let him forget that, either.

"Sorry," she mumbled.

He looked to see what she meant. She'd noticed him gawking at her, all right. She fixed the robe to cover her breasts but then licked the sugar off her fingers.

Yeah, he was definitely toast.

He wasn't sure why she was having this effect on him now. Maybe it was because he was pushing through the rest of the adrenaline crash. Or if he was truthful with himself, Jaycee had always had this effect on him.

Well, before the shooting that nearly killed him anyway.

Josh had been able to use that incident to keep the heat at bay, but he was failing miserably at it right now.

"Sorry," she mumbled again. And yep, she'd noticed that he was practically drooling over her.

He muttered some profanity and moved away from her. "I think I'll go ahead and grab a shower." An ice-cold one to chill him down. Maybe two of them.

But she stood and blocked his path.

A really bad idea.

The last thing he needed right now was to be close to her. Even if that was exactly what he wanted.

"I don't want this to be an issue between us." She licked her lips this time, no doubt searching for any stray sugar bits left over from the doughnut, and she was driving him crazy in the process. "The attraction was always there. *Always*," she repeated when he gave her a flat look.

Yeah, it had been.

And it still was.

It took Josh several seconds to repeat the bad stuff that'd gone on between them. Several more seconds to drill it into his brain that while he did forgive her, crossing the line with her now could be dangerous.

Did that stop him?

Nope.

With the sane part of him yelling for him to stop, he reached out, sliding his hand right into that robe, and he found exactly what his body was looking for.

A warm, soft, naked woman who could burn him to ash.

Even though she'd been the one to stop him from leaving the room, Jaycee suddenly got that deer-caught-in-headlights look. "Uh, you're sure about this?"

At least that was what Josh thought she said. He couldn't be certain because he kissed her before she finished talking. Still, he caught the gist of what she meant. Like him,

Jaycee knew the timing for this sucked. And not just the timing—everything about this was wrong, wrong, wrong.

That didn't stop him, either.

He just kept kissing her. Kept sliding his hand deeper into the robe until he was cupping her breast. He swiped his thumb over her nipple and got a very good reaction.

Or bad, depending on perspective.

From his insane body's perspective, it was the right reaction. She moaned, that little silky sound of pleasure, and she melted against him.

She tasted sweet, like the sugary doughnut, but it was mixed with something else. Something dark and forbidden.

Which she was.

But that only made the kiss hotter. It only made him want her more.

He shoved open the robe. He'd been right about the naked part. Not a stitch of clothes, and he broke the kiss just long enough to look at her.

Yeah, he'd also been right about the burning-to-ash part.

Before he could talk himself out of it, he backed her against the counter. He didn't think beyond the moment of pleasuring her. Pleasuring himself by touching her. And his hand was already sliding between her legs when he got a quick slap back to reality.

The baby.

Or rather her pregnant belly.

He shook his head, hoping to clear it. Didn't work. And he opened his mouth to ask a question that he shouldn't ask.

Was it okay for them to be doing this?

Of course, the answer was *no*. It wasn't okay, but since his body wasn't going to listen to that, he needed to know if it was physically okay for them to be doing this.

He got his answer fast.

Jaycee kissed him, pulling him right back to her. "There's no reason to stop because of the baby. It's okay for pregnant women to have sex."

There went his out. Because there were only two things that could have stopped him from jumping off this cliff— Jaycee saying no or her telling him she couldn't continue because of the baby. But clearly she didn't want an out, either.

And Josh didn't give her one.

He shoved open her robe and dropped some kisses on her neck. Then her breasts, which were full and warm and smelled sweet like the rest of her. Each touch of his mouth caused her to make those silky sounds of pleasure.

So Josh kept going.

Kept kissing until the fire was burning too hot inside him. He was pretty sure it was burning inside her, too, because she kept fighting to get closer.

"The bed," Jaycee managed to say. She pulled him up, kissing his mouth and maneuvering him in that direction.

She had the right idea about the bed, but it was taking way too long to get there. Everything was taking too long. Because his body kept hammering home that he needed her *now*.

Without breaking the kiss, Josh scooped her up, took her across the room and eased her onto the bed. He reminded himself to stay gentle.

But Jaycee didn't help with that, either.

The moment her back touched the mattress, she hooked her arm around his neck and pulled him on top of her. He kept most of his weight on his forearms, but Jaycee took full advantage of the gap between their bodies, and she unbuttoned his shirt. It involved a lot of touching, and when she shucked it off him, her clever hands went to his bare chest.

Stomach.

And lower.

To the front of his jeans.

Oh, man. Josh hadn't thought the fire inside could get any hotter, but he'd been wrong. That did it. When he got his eyes uncrossed, he stood just long enough the rid himself of his boots and jeans. He would have gotten to his boxers next, but Jaycee reared up to help him.

More eye crossing.

Either she wasn't very good at taking off a man's underwear or else she wanted to torture him. Josh didn't have time to decide which because she pulled him back onto the bed with her.

"Let's finish this," she insisted.

He did. Josh eased into her, and he had to bite back some profanity because she felt that good. That slick heat only made him need her more.

And that need was yelling for him to finish her *now*.

Part of him wished he could savor this moment, but that part of him lost the battle fast. Jaycee saw to that. She wrapped her arms and legs around him, pushing him deeper inside her. And faster. Until she could take no more.

The climax rippled through her body, and Josh watched the pleasure of her release spread across her face. She touched her tongue to her top lip. Closed her eyes.

Whispered his name.

Josh didn't even try to speak. Didn't try to hold on for one last moment of pleasure.

He just let himself fall.

Chapter Sixteen

Jaycee just wanted to lie there in bed and enjoy every bit of this moment.

But Josh obviously had different plans.

He eased off her as if she was delicate crystal that might shatter beneath him, and he dropped on his back beside her. His breathing was still heavy, the pulse jumping on his throat, but because he was staring up at the ceiling, she could no longer look into his eyes.

Which was just as well.

Right before he'd moved, Jaycee had caught a glimpse of his "what the heck have I done?" expression. She'd expected it, of course. Because part of her felt the same way.

Probably not for the same reason as Josh, however.

What she'd told him was true—she always had been attracted to him. That's why she'd fallen so easily into bed with him five months ago. However, deeper down, it had felt like more than a mere attraction.

And that scared the heck out of her.

Josh had told her that he hadn't considered himself father material because of his parents' messy divorce when he was a kid. Well, she didn't consider herself relationship material because of messy parents, either.

Yet here she was. In bed with Josh again. Complicating both their lives.

Still, she didn't regret it.

Even if she should.

He groaned. Not quite as bad as the groan he'd made five months ago when he had learned she was in part responsible for his partner's death and his own injury. She turned to him, ready to apologize—just to get it out of the way—but he leaned over and dropped a kiss on her mouth.

"I moved back to Silver Creek because I thought it'd be safer," he grumbled. "Ironic, huh?"

She thought about that a moment. "Are you talking about me, the baby or the gun-slinging guards?"

He turned his head, snagged her gaze. "Definitely not the baby." And he planted another kiss on her belly. "The guards, for sure. You, well, you're dangerous in your own way."

Jaycee cringed and pushed aside the memories of his shooting. Playtime was apparently over. Reality and their painful pasts were back. She pulled the sides of the robe over her naked body and started to get up.

She didn't make it far.

Josh pulled her right back down with him.

"I wasn't talking about the shooting five months ago," he clarified. He slipped his arm beneath her and brought her closer to him. "It's hard for me to concentrate around you."

She looked down his body at the part of him that'd been very hard just minutes earlier, and she smiled. Yes, it was stupid. She didn't have much to smile about, except this was the most relaxed and satisfied her body had felt in five months.

Since the last time Josh and she had been together.

Jaycee levered herself up a little so she could make eye contact with him. She wanted him to see the determined look on her face when she gave him an out that he obviously wanted. He'd certainly wanted one five months ago.

"This doesn't have to mean anything," she said. *There*. It was the perfect out.

Except she didn't get quite the reaction she'd thought she would from him. Josh frowned. "I was about to ask you to marry me."

She sucked in her breath so fast that Jaycee got choked on it. Jaycee couldn't even repeat what he'd said, much less answer it. "You've lost your mind," she managed to say after several moments.

"Probably. But neither of us had the chance to be raised by two parents. We could give that to her...our child."

Jaycee froze again. Josh was really throwing the surprises at her tonight.

"It's a girl?" she asked.

But he didn't confirm or deny it. "You said you didn't want to know."

"I said I didn't want to know right then, when I was ready to jump out of my skin. I don't feel that way now."

He only shook his head and gave her a naughty-boy smile. "Just consider it a slip of the tongue. Now, back to my proposal—"

"My answer's no," Jaycee interrupted.

That brought him to a sitting position, and every trace of his smile vanished. "No?"

"No," she repeated. She sat up, too, and looked him straight in the eyes. "We can both raise our daughter, or our son," Jaycee amended, "and we can do that without being married."

"How? With me here and you over in San Antonio? I know it's not that far, but sooner or later you'll want to go back to work."

Yes, and she'd thought Josh would do the same. "Does that mean you're staying here in Silver Creek?"

"Possibly. Probably," he amended several seconds later. "The deputy job feels right, you know. So does being around family."

No, she didn't know, and her silence must have told Josh that he'd hit a nerve. "You love your job as an agent," he added.

"Do I?" She hadn't intended to say that aloud, but with it out there, she just continued to bare her soul that she probably should keep covered. "I always thought I had to work twice as hard to prove myself."

"Because of your parents," he finished for her. "But you love it?" And that time it was a question.

"Parts of it. Like finding justice for people who might not get it any other way." That was what she'd always believed, but she slid her hand over her stomach.

The baby had changed everything.

It had changed *her.*

Jaycee couldn't see herself kissing her baby goodbye each morning while she went out and dodged bullets for the rest of the day.

When had this happened? When had she turned into something she'd always believed she wouldn't become? A soon-to-be mother. One who'd just minutes earlier offered Josh joint custody. Apparently, a good round of sex had caused her to have a dull brain, because she hadn't even made up her mind about that.

"I'll look for a different job," she finally said. "Maybe one here in town so that distance wouldn't be a problem."

"Marriage might make things easier."

"Or harder," she argued. Jaycee huffed. "The sex will only take us so far if we stay under the same roof. Sooner or later, we'd have to deal with the issues that drove us apart five months ago."

He stared at her. Didn't dispute that. Nor did he verbally withdraw his proposal.

However, Jaycee could see the withdrawal in his eyes.

She could see the pain, too, and she was responsible for a lot of that. Since she doubted he wanted to discuss that pain, she brought up the other bombshell he'd dropped.

"So is it a boy or a girl?" she asked.

He opened his mouth, and Jaycee thought she might finally get an answer to her question.

But she didn't.

His phone rang, and after she saw Grayson's name on the screen, she knew it was a call he'd have to take. Thankfully, he put it on speaker so she could hear.

"The blood tests on Sierra's baby just came back," Grayson started, "and Bryson's not the father."

Jaycee shook her head. "They can determine that from blood tests?"

"They can if they know the blood types of the parents. Sierra's is type A, and Bryson's type O. That means the baby has to be either A or O to be their child, but the baby's type B. The baby had to have gotten that blood type from her biological father."

And that was something they might never find out. Well, unless Sierra could figure out how to use it to her advantage. "So Sierra faked the amnio test results?"

"Looks that way, and Bryson's not going to be too happy about it."

"He knows?" Josh asked.

"Not yet. I'm calling him next. I'll let you know how it goes."

"Bryson's going to be furious," Jaycee mumbled, but she was thankful that the man wouldn't get custody of the child. Still, she wasn't sure the baby would fare much better with Sierra. Or even the real birth father.

And speaking of babies, that reminded Jaycee of what Josh and she had been discussing before Grayson's call. The sex of their own baby.

"I want to know," Jaycee insisted. But again, no answer.

The lights went out, plunging them into total darkness.

JOSH WENT STILL for several seconds. And listened. Waiting for the power to come back on.

It didn't.

It wasn't unusual for the electricity to go off during storms, but there was no storm outside. Not the kind created by Mother Nature anyway.

He got up from the bed and dressed. Fast. Jaycee did the same, and he hurried to the window to look out. The main house was dark, too, and so were the exterior security lights and Grayson's house. So not just a power outage at his place but what appeared to be the entire ranch.

His phone rang, and he reached for both it and his gun. "Grayson," he answered after seeing his name on the screen. "What's going on?"

"Not sure, but Gage and I are heading out to check on it now. Stay with Jaycee. The security system will kick over to battery power so we should know if someone breaches the fence or the houses."

Including his apartment, since it was on the same security grid.

Josh hated to put his cousins in possible harm's way again, but protecting Jaycee had to be his priority, so he'd definitely stay put.

And keep watch.

Jaycee did the same on the other side of the window after she took his gun from the top of his fridge.

"I don't see anyone. Do you?" she asked.

No more heat in her voice. Just fear that caused her words to tremble a little. Something he hated to hear because lately fear had been there way too often.

He shook his head. Kept watching. And not just the area in front of the barn. Josh watched the sides, too.

Of course, he had one big blind spot because there were no windows at the back of his apartment. If anyone did come in from the pasture or the back road, he wouldn't be able to see them until they got to the exterior stairs that led up to his place.

He saw some movement near the main house. Ranch hands, probably. They didn't head his way but fanned out, staying close to the house. No doubt looking for anyone who might be a threat. Too bad there were plenty who could fall into that threat category since there was still a decorating crew on the grounds.

Jaycee was breathing through her mouth now, her breath fogging up the glass. Thanks to the moonlight, he could see her face. Could see the terror there and the death grip she had on the gun.

Josh was about to reassure her that it was probably nothing.

But he saw *something*.

Or at least he thought he did.

"What's wrong?" she asked, her gaze frantically searching the grounds below.

Josh didn't answer. He focused all his attention near the stairs where he thought he'd spotted some kind of movement, but no one was there. At least no one in his line of sight.

However, there were plenty of places for someone to hide.

He kept watching. Kept waiting. And he cursed the

stress that Jaycee had to be feeling by now. If it was only partially as high as his, then it was too much. Not just for her but for the baby.

Just when he thought he could release the breath that he'd been holding, Josh saw it again. The shadow at the base of the stairs. He hoped it was just the moonlight playing tricks with his eyes and the wooden railing.

No such luck.

The shadow moved again.

And he saw that it was a man dressed all in black. He also got a glimpse of the gun he was holding.

One of the guards from the baby farm, no doubt.

"Move away from the window," Josh ordered Jaycee. "And get on the floor."

While she hurried to do that, Josh took out his phone to call Grayson, but the man in black starting running up the stairs.

He wasn't alone.

There were two others following him.

"Get under the bed," Josh told Jaycee. No time to do much else.

He could hear the footsteps thundering on the stairs, and he pivoted and took aim at the door.

Just as one of the men kicked it in.

There was the cracking sound of the wood, and the door slamming into the wall. Then the security system. Not a blare yet, but a steady beeping sound to give him time to punch in the code to stop the alarm from going off. Josh wouldn't do that. He wanted the alarm. Wanted everyone on the ranch alerted that he had an intruder.

Josh held his fire, waiting for them to step inside.

But that didn't happen.

Through the frantic beeps of the security system, he

heard another sound of something metal hitting the floor. Unfortunately, this sound was familiar.

A tear-gas canister.

Not just one of them but three.

It didn't take long, just a few seconds, for the milky-white gas to start billowing through the room. And to reach Jaycee and him. They started coughing, and Josh's eyes burned like fire. He couldn't see, and he couldn't risk shooting because he didn't want to hit Jaycee.

The alarm came. Full blast. The sound vibrated through the room and through his head.

Josh ran to Jaycee, groping to find her in the darkness. He tried to shield her with his body, but he couldn't stay standing. The coughing and burning took over, and he couldn't catch his breath. He had no choice but to drop to his knees.

He heard movement to his right. Tried to take aim at the dark figures moving through the cloud of gas. He got just a glimpse of one of them wearing a mask.

Before the guy bashed the butt of a rifle against Josh's head.

The pain exploded through him, and even though he tried to fight back, he dropped like deadweight onto the floor.

Jaycee made a sound. A strangled scream that he heard even over the piercing alarm. Josh tried to get up. To fight back so he could protect her. But another blow to his head put him right back down on the floor.

A shot blasted through the room, causing his fear to snowball out of control. "Jaycee?" he managed to say.

But she didn't answer.

Oh, God.

Had she been shot? Or was she the one who'd done the firing?

Josh couldn't tell, but he heard another clanging sound and got a glimpse of a gun falling to the floor next to him. He couldn't be sure, but he thought it was the same gun that Jaycee had been carrying.

"No!" Jaycee said through the coughing and wheezing. And she just kept repeating it.

One of the mask-wearing men scooped her up, giving Josh a hard kick to the chest in the process. Another jolt of pain, but despite the searing pain and the tear gas, he didn't stay down. He fought to get up and stumbled across the room toward the still-open door.

He had to get to her.

Had to stop these men and save her.

Though it seemed to take an eternity, Josh made it to the doorway. And he took aim. But the men had already made it all the way down the stairs and were heading toward the rear of the barn.

"Stop!" Josh yelled. He knew they wouldn't listen, but he hoped to alert some of the ranch hands. There were several already running his way.

He was dizzy, still fighting to breathe and see, but Josh got down the stairs. Running as fast as he could. But he heard two more sounds that he didn't want to hear.

Jaycee's scream.

And the engine of a vehicle starting up.

There were several vehicles parked back there for the ranch hands to use, but he doubted any ranch hand was behind the wheel. No.

It was one of the guards.

Josh took aim, praying he'd be able to shoot out the tires. But the truck didn't come his way. He caught just a glimpse of the bloodred taillights as the truck sped across the pasture.

With Jaycee inside.

Chapter Seventeen

Jaycee fought as if her life depended on it.

Because it did.

Her life, the baby's and Josh's were all hanging in the balance. She'd seen the way the goon had kicked Josh and bashed him with a gun. Jaycee prayed he wasn't hurt. Or worse. And while she was praying, she added one for her to get away from these monsters.

It wasn't working.

No matter how hard she fought or how loud she screamed, it didn't help. The hulking scumbags just held on to her and shoved her into a truck a split second before it sped away. They peeled off their gas masks, tossing them on the truck floor, but it was hard to see their faces because they were covered in camouflage paint.

She kept blinking her eyes, trying to focus even though they were still stinging and watery from the tear gas. But she finally got just a glimpse of Josh in the side mirror. He was running toward her like a madman, and he had his gun aimed but didn't shoot.

Couldn't.

Because he wouldn't risk hitting her.

Her heart went to her stomach as the truck drove away and Josh disappeared from sight. This couldn't be happening. She couldn't go through this again.

She tried to push aside the fear and the dread and concentrate on what she could do. Not much with three armed goons squeezed into the truck with her. It was a two-seater vehicle, and one of the guys was in the back, a gun pointed at her head. She was on the front seat sandwiched between the other two.

Jaycee reached between the driver and her, hoping to snag a weapon he had in his pocket, but the other two jerks stopped her before her hand even made it to the man. The one on her right cursed her, calling her a bad name, and he grabbed the seat belt and buckled her up.

"Who are you and what do you want?" she demanded, and Jaycee hoped she sounded like an FBI agent and not a terrified pregnant woman.

None of them answered. In fact, the two in the front seat didn't even spare her a glance. The driver had his attention on the rocky dirt road, and the one in the passenger's seat was looking in the side mirror. No doubt looking for whoever would follow them.

And someone would follow.

Josh, no doubt, and she prayed he didn't get himself killed while trying to rescue her again.

The goon in the passenger seat didn't take his eyes off the side mirror, but he made a call. Because he sheltered his hand over the phone, Jaycee couldn't see the numbers that he pressed in, and she didn't hear who answered over the noise of her heartbeat crashing in her ears. However, she did hear his single-sentence response.

"We have her."

So none of these three were in charge. They were just minions for the person who was no doubt responsible for the baby farms.

Jaycee couldn't go back there.

She looked around the cab of the truck for anything she

could use as a weapon. The discarded gas masks were on the floor, and if she could grab one she could wallop one of them with it. Of course, the other two would just stop her attack.

Or they might crash.

A crash *might* get her free of them, but it was a huge risk to take.

So what could she do to get away from them?

Normally, she'd try negotiation, but Jaycee seriously doubted that would work with these three. No. They were on a mission to take her to someone who would do heaven knows what with her baby and her.

She had a very short list of things she could try to get herself out of this mess. And next up was some old-fashioned deception. She clutched her stomach and moaned as loudly as she could.

"The baby," she yelled. "Oh, God. The baby! I think I'm miscarrying."

Just as she'd hoped, that got their attention. The two in the front seat exchanged concerned glances, and the goon on her right took out his phone to make another call.

"She's making a fuss about the baby," he said to the person on the other end of the line. "I'm pretty sure she's faking it, but better get the doctor out there just in case."

Jaycee wished she could reach through the line and crush the person her captor was talking to, because he or she had almost certainly orchestrated all of this. She seriously doubted she'd get to see the culprit though because this dirtbag was a coward, letting the hired muscle do the kidnapping.

The guy put his phone away again. And he cursed. For a moment Jaycee thought she was the reason for the renewed profanity, but she followed his gaze to the side mirror.

There were headlights behind them in the distance.

It was an SUV, and it looked like the one that'd been parked behind the barn.

Josh.

Maybe he'd brought a family full of backup with him.

She kept up the moaning and arched her back so that her elbows jabbed into the men on each side of her. They didn't seem to notice, and the one in the backseat swiveled around and took aim. Not at her but at the person trying to rescue her. There was a small slide window that was open so the idiot goons would likely have a good shot.

Jaycee needed to do something about that.

She upped the volume on her moaning and levered herself up even higher when she pretended to have a contraction. In the same motion, Jaycee threw back her hand, knocking into the arm of the man in the rear seat. Now he cursed her and raised his left hand as if he might slap her.

"Keep your eyes on the SUV behind us," the driver snarled.

Even in the dim light, she saw the anger flash in the guard's eyes, but he turned back around and pointed his gun again.

Now Jaycee cursed.

She'd failed.

And worse, the guy fired a shot at the SUV. Not one shot but two. She couldn't tell if he'd hit anything, but she prayed Josh and anyone else inside were all right.

The truck bobbled over a rough patch of road, and the driver had to give the wheel a sharp turn to the left to stop them from going into the ditch. Behind him, the other vehicle gained some ground. Probably because the driver was familiar with every inch of this road and the guard wasn't. Her captor practically had to slam on his brakes when they reached a sharp turn.

Jaycee saw another of those sharp curves ahead, and

she held her breath, waiting for the driver to slow down so he could safely take the turn. Anything she did at this point was a huge risk, but so was just sitting there while the idiot behind her continued to pop off shots at the SUV.

Shots that could hit Josh.

When the driver slowed as much as she figured he'd slow for the curve, Jaycee drew back her elbow and rammed it as hard as she could into his ribs.

He howled in pain.

The other one in the passenger's seat reached for her, but she grabbed a gas mask and bashed first him, then the other. More howling. And the truck did more than just bobble. It went into a skid.

From the corner of her eye, she saw the guy in the back turn his gun on her, and her heart went into overdrive. He was going to shoot her.

But he didn't get a chance to fire.

The truck skidded right off the road, hurling them over some rocks and shrubs. Jaycee's head hit the ceiling, and the guards and she bobbled around like rag dolls.

Ahead she saw the tree, but there was nothing she could do except shelter her stomach with her hands.

They plowed right into a sprawling oak.

JOSH'S BREATH VANISHED when he saw the truck leave the road. He figured the driver had lost control, but then he could see some kind of struggle going on in the cab.

Hell.

If Jaycee was hurt, every one of those men would pay for it.

Josh pulled his SUV to a stop and barreled out. Grayson and a ranch hand weren't too far behind him, but he didn't want to wait for them. He had to make sure Jaycee was all right.

His head was still pounding. So was the pain in his chest where the kidnapper had kicked him. But Josh fought through the pain, jumped the ditch and ran full speed toward the collision.

The truck was wrecked, no doubt about that, and there was steam spewing from the hood, which was now smashed against the tree.

The driver's door flew open, and the man practically spilled out. He was armed, but he didn't take the time to turn around and aim at Josh. He just raced behind a big clump of rocks and dropped to the ground.

Not good.

Josh ducked, darted behind a tree. The passenger's side door opened, too, and he braced himself to see scumbags number two and three.

However, it was Jaycee who crawled out.

Not easily. She climbed over one of the men, who appeared to be only partly conscious. He was moaning and cursing at the same time, but Jaycee managed to get by him. The moment her feet touched the ground, she ran toward him.

Josh caught her in his arms and pulled her behind the tree with him. He didn't kiss her. Didn't want to take his attention off that truck and the kidnappers, but he was beyond thankful that she hadn't been hurt.

"You're okay," he managed to say at the same time that Jaycee said it to him.

"I was wearing a seat belt," she added. "They weren't."

Thank heaven for that, and Josh added a wish that the trio was hurt too badly to put up much of a fight.

His wish didn't come true.

A bullet smashed right into the tree, just inches from where Jaycee and he were standing. Josh pushed her against the rough bark, protecting her as best he could with his body, and he glanced out to see what was going on.

Scumbag number one had been the person to fire the shot. Scumbags two and three were climbing out on the driver's side. Away from Jaycee and him.

Which meant Josh didn't have a good shot at any of them.

Three guns to one weren't good odds. Especially when all three of them opened fire. The shots blasted into the tree.

"Give me your backup weapon from your boot holster," Jaycee insisted.

But Josh had to shake his head. "I don't have it." Because he'd literally had to throw on his clothes after the power had been cut.

"How about a knife, anything?" she pressed.

There was no knife or anything else he could give to Jaycee. Only himself. And that had to be enough, because he wasn't willing to deal with the alternative of her being taken captive again.

Josh looked behind him and saw truck lights slash through the darkness. His backup was on the way, but it was dangerous for Grayson to drive straight into a hail of bullets. He handed Jaycee his phone.

"Text Grayson." He had to yell over the noise from the shots so she could hear him. "Let him know where we are and that he needs to stay back until they stop shooting."

Josh wanted backup now, but it'd be suicide for Grayson to come driving into this.

Jaycee sent the text and shoved his phone back into his pocket. Josh fired off a single shot at the gunmen just so they'd know he was armed and so they wouldn't try to come closer.

Just up the narrow dirt road, Grayson stopped his truck,

but he kept the headlights on. It was a like a beacon for the kidnappers because they sent some of the shots in that direction. Josh hoped his cousin and the ranch hand stayed down. Sooner or later these idiots were going to run out of ammunition.

He hoped.

Then Josh could make his move. He wasn't sure exactly what his move would be, but he needed to get Jaycee far away from these men who'd kidnapped her.

It'd been a brazen attack. The kind that only dangerous criminals would attempt, and he had to do everything humanly possible to make sure they didn't get their hands back on her.

His phone dinged, indicating he had a text message, and Josh motioned for Jaycee to read it. "Grayson says he's going to create a diversion. His brothers are closing off the other end of the road."

So the kidnappers would be trapped. That was good. He wanted them trapped and caught, but Josh wasn't so sure about this diversion.

"What diversion?" he asked Jaycee. But she didn't have time to answer.

"Put down your weapons!" Grayson shouted.

Of course, the men didn't listen. That only caused them to fire more shots in Grayson's direction. Josh wondered if this was a ploy to make them use up the ammunition even faster, but then he saw Grayson's truck.

It was creeping along, headed not toward Jaycee and him but right toward the clump of rocks that the men were using for cover.

Not a bad diversion.

Josh put his mouth against Jaycee's ear. "When the truck gets between us and the men, we move."

She gave a shaky nod. Actually, everything about her

was shaky, and he hoped she hadn't lied about being okay. It seemed to take an eternity for the truck to reach them, and the gunmen cursed it and kept shooting. When it gave Jaycee and him the best possible cover, he caught on to her hand and got her moving.

They'd only made it a few steps before the shots came right at them.

Chapter Eighteen

Jaycee kept as low as she could and kept running.

Thanks to Josh.

He had hold of her arm, and he didn't let go despite the bullets kicking up dirt and rocks all around them. He pulled her onto the other side of a dirt embankment, and they dropped to the ground.

There were more shots.

But not all were coming from the kidnappers.

Some were coming from the direction of the dirt road where she'd last seen Grayson and another man. A ranch hand, most likely. Jaycee had caught only a glimpse of them before their truck had started moving their way. Now that truck had run into the clump of rocks where the kidnappers had taken cover.

At least one of the men was hurt. She'd gotten a glimpse of the blood on his face before she had crawled over him and escaped. Jaycee hoped his wounds were bad enough that he couldn't return fire and also so that his comrades would want to get him out of there fast and to a hospital. They would have to stop shooting to do that, and then maybe Grayson and Josh could move in to arrest them.

The shots kept coming, but they weren't aimed directly at her. Most of the shots were going to the left, the bullets tearing through the dirt and scattering the debris every-

where, including her eyes. She was still feeling the effects
of the tear gas, and the debris and the darkness didn't help.

That thought froze in her head.

Not the debris. But the tear gas.

Oh, mercy. Could that have harmed the baby?

She slid her hand over her stomach and prayed that it
hadn't, but it made the situation even more urgent. She,
too, needed to get to a hospital. Of course, these men would
try to stop that from happening. Clearly, this was still a
kidnapping attempt.

And she still didn't know why.

Was it because she was an FBI agent and they wanted
to find out what she'd learned? Or did they only want the
baby? Jaycee hoped she found out soon because that answer might give her some clues as to who was behind this.

Josh was already practically on top of her. Sheltering
and protecting her. And as before, he put his mouth right
against her ear.

"The ranch road curves and continues over there," he
said, tipping his head to a heavily treed area on the right.
"If we can get there, someone can pick us up and get us
out of here."

Jaycee was all for that, though moving would mean
leaving cover. For a few seconds anyway.

"Send Grayson another text," Josh added. "See if he
can create another diversion and tell him we're going to
move to the road away from the shooters. Have him get
someone out there if he can."

Her hands were shaking like crazy, but Jaycee managed
to write the text. And the waiting began. The kidnappers
kept shooting, but from what she could tell, they weren't
moving in for the kill.

Why not?

She shook her head, glad that it wasn't happening but wondering what the heck they were waiting for.

Or who.

Maybe their boss hadn't given them an out—they weren't to come back unless they had her.

Josh's phone dinged, and she saw the response text from Grayson. Will do.

Grayson didn't give details, but a moment later, she saw the plan in action. A hot pink flare shot into the night sky like fireworks. But not just into the sky. Several of the flares came shooting like rockets right at the kidnappers.

Josh didn't wait to see what would happen. He got them moving again away from the embankment and to those trees. It took a few seconds, just enough time for them to reach cover, before the shots came their way again.

The second diversion had worked.

Well, for Josh and her anyway.

With the new position, she was able to see the shooter, and two were firing at Grayson. The other, at Josh and her.

So much for hoping that one guy was injured too badly to fire.

All three men looked fit and ready to kill. And they were sending most of their shots at Grayson. She hoped he'd taken cover before shooting off those flares.

"Let's go," Josh said over the deafening noise, and that was the only warning Jaycee got before he moved them to another tree. Then another.

Each step was a huge risk because the shots kept coming—not directly at her but at Josh and the others. Even when one of the men stopped to reload, his partners picked up the slack and just continued firing.

Josh and she worked their way through the trees, and she tried to position herself so the men wouldn't be able to shoot him. But Josh would have no part in that. He just shoved her right back behind him and continued their trek to the road.

So did one of the kidnappers.

The bulky one who'd driven the truck moved out from behind the rocks and came after them.

That sent her heart crashing against her ribs, but it didn't slow them down. Even when the guy fired into the tree they were using for cover, Josh just kept them moving toward the road.

It seemed to take an eternity before Jaycee finally saw the dirt road just ahead.

She also saw the kidnapper behind them.

Josh did, too. He leaned out, sent a bullet the man's way, but the guy just briefly ducked out of sight. The snake used the same trees for cover that Josh and she had.

"Wait," Josh said to her, and he stopped several yards from the road.

It was much darker in this area because the towering trees on both sides blocked most of the moonlight. Her eyes had already adjusted to the darkness, but she could hardly see anything.

Certainly no headlights from a rescue vehicle.

"We'll follow the road until someone from the ranch gets here," Josh explained.

Jaycee had no idea how long it would take for a vehicle to circle back around to this point, but she prayed it wouldn't take long.

Josh got them moving again. Not on the road itself but along the side of it. Probably so they could still use the trees for cover if things got worse.

Without the gunshots blasting nearby, she could hear the kidnapper clomping his way through the woods. She couldn't tell how far away he was, but he was close.

Too close.

Once the rescue car arrived, he might be able to kill
Josh and anyone else who got in his way.

The road made another of those sharp curves, and Josh
slowed when they made it around the curve and came out
onto a straight stretch.

"Hell," she heard him mumble, and he pulled her to
the ground.

It took Jaycee a moment to figure out why he'd done
that.

And then she saw it.

The car.

No headlights, and it was black, blending right into the
murky darkness.

The driver's-side door opened, and she held her breath.
Hoping it was someone from the ranch there to rescue
them. But her heart went to her knees when she saw the
camouflage clothes.

Identical to those the other kidnappers were wearing.

Josh fired at the man.

Just as the man fired at them.

JOSH PULLED JAYCEE back down again. Not a second too
soon. Because his shot missed the guy, and the bullet that
came their way slammed into the tree just above their
heads.

Or rather *his* head.

The scumbags didn't seem to be aiming for Jaycee. That
was the good news. The bad news was the bullets were
still coming damn close, and she could be hit.

Three more shots came his way. Plus one from the guy
following them from behind.

Jaycee and he were trapped in the middle.

The flashbacks came, of course. And Josh cursed them.

He didn't have time for this, but they came anyway. Images of another shooting.

Of his partner lying dead in a pool of blood.

Of the shots slamming into Josh's chest.

He pushed them aside and hoped he could keep them at bay. Jaycee's life might depend on that.

"This is over," the one by the car said. He'd taken cover behind the door, and it was too dark for Josh to tell if he was alone or if anyone was inside.

He was betting someone was in there.

Maybe the scumbags' boss.

But Josh figured Jaycee and he wouldn't get that lucky. So far, he'd sucked in the luck department.

"If you want to live," the guy added, "you'll put down your gun now."

Josh was pretty sure that wasn't the way to stay alive. Without his gun, the men would just have an easier time killing him and kidnapping Jaycee.

He looked around, trying to find someplace that Jaycee and he could use for cover. Preferably something to his right so he could keep an eye on the two armed men and anyone who might be in that car.

Josh finally spotted something.

A fallen tree that'd just missed hitting the road. It was huge, the trunk at least two feet thick, and it was only about four yards away. If they could get to that, it would give him a better position to take out at least one of the gunmen.

But they could just gun him down before he got a chance to do that.

He considered another plan. One that he hated because it would test his theory that they didn't want Jaycee dead. Only him.

"What are you thinking?" she asked, following his gaze to that tree trunk.

He could no longer see her face as well as he had by the embankment, but he could hear the terror in her voice. Yes, she was a trained agent, but she didn't have a gun, and she was no doubt worried about the baby. And also worried about what would happen if those men got their hands on her.

"What?" she pressed. "I'll do whatever it takes to get us out of here."

He believed her, but she still wasn't going to like what he had in mind. Hell, he didn't like it much, either. However, it might keep Jaycee alive. Of course, he didn't want her kept alive just so she could be kidnapped.

"Text Grayson again," Josh whispered to her. "See if he can get someone to the back road where we are. Tell him we're near the big fallen tree."

She nodded, her fingers flying over the buttons on his phone, and he heard the little sound to indicate the text had been sent.

Now the waiting began.

It was eerily quiet. No one was shooting at them, and he didn't know how long the pair would just hang around until they closed in on them.

"You heard that part about me telling you to drop your gun," the guy by the car said. Then he said something over his shoulder.

To the person inside the car.

So he did have help. Help that would no doubt spring to life the moment they had Josh in their kill zone.

And that was about to happen soon.

The guy behind them was moving closer. Getting into position so he could shoot and not hit Jaycee. Only Josh.

"What happens if I put down my gun?" Josh asked. He didn't really want an answer. He knew. But he needed a little time for Grayson to answer.

The guy said something over his shoulder again and stayed crouched behind the car door, making it next to impossible to shoot him. "Put down your gun and we'll talk."

Right. Just talk. Josh figured there was no chance of that happening.

"Jaycee's right next to me," Josh reminded them. "If you shoot me, you could hurt her. Or worse."

It wasn't easy saying that, and it felt as if someone had clamped a big meaty fist around his heart. Still, he'd say or do anything to keep her alive, and he was bargaining on the armed pair feeling the same way.

Finally, he heard the soft dinging sound to indicate they had an answer to the text. "Grayson said the road's blocked by another vehicle, but Gage is coming to us on foot."

Good. Well, good about Gage. The other vehicle bothered him a lot. He hoped like the devil that there weren't more armed men inside.

"I want you to move over there," Josh told her, tipping his head to the tree trunk. "Move fast. Then get down and stay put."

She shook her head. "But what about you? Where will you be?"

Now here was the part she wouldn't like. "I'm staying here. I want to take out at least one of these idiots."

She pulled in her breath. Stared at him. "But if I move away, they'll shoot you."

Yeah. No way to sugarcoat that. "I'm a good shot," Josh reminded her. It was true. But he wasn't good enough to take out two men standing at different locations at the same time.

Though he couldn't see her eyes, he could feel the argument coming on, and he wanted to nip it in the bud. "You have to think of the baby."

Josh hadn't wanted to play the baby card, but he figured that was the only chance he had of getting her to agree to this plan.

"Just do it," he pressed. "It won't be long before Gage is here to help."

At least he hoped that was true.

"We can wait for Gage," she insisted.

But they couldn't. They were already on borrowed time, and the scumbag behind them was closing in. Inch by inch. Soon, he'd be close enough to pick Josh off.

And that would leave Jaycee unarmed and unprotected.

Josh brushed a kiss on her lips. "Please, just do it."

"Time's up," the kidnapper said.

It was. The guy behind him was in position, and Josh could see him ready to take aim.

"Go now!" Josh ordered Jaycee.

Maybe it was the sheer volume of his voice, but she finally moved. She scrambled toward the tree trunk, and Josh pivoted and took aim at the guy behind him.

He fired, a double tap of the trigger.

And hit him.

Josh didn't watch to see if he fell. If the guy wasn't dead, he at least wouldn't be able to return fire anyway. From the corner of his eye, he saw Jaycee drop to the other side of the tree truck.

Out of the line of fire.

However, Josh wasn't.

The gunman by the car pulled the trigger, and the bullet slammed right into Josh.

Chapter Nineteen

This was the repeat of a nightmare that Jaycee had already had way too often. Josh being shot and her being the reason for it. Now here it was again, playing out in the dark woods. But it wasn't a nightmare.

It was real.

So was the bullet that'd hit Josh.

Jaycee didn't think. She needed only to get to him to make sure he was alive. She ran to him, slinging her arm around him to steady him, but Josh only tried to push her behind him.

"You're hurt," she told him, just in case he was in shock and hadn't realized it.

But no shock. He glared at her and stepped in front of her. "You should have stayed behind the tree trunk," Josh said through clenched teeth.

"You've been shot," she repeated.

"I'm okay."

He darn sure didn't look okay. Jaycee saw the gaping tear on his shirtsleeve and his arm. The blood looked black and shiny in the darkness and was already seeping through the fabric.

"What the deputy's trying to tell you," the gunman calmly said, "is that I gave him a superficial wound to draw you out. I kept him alive so you'd cooperate."

Oh, mercy.

Jaycee had been too crazy with worry to consider that. And it'd worked.

Well, it'd gotten her out from cover anyway, but she couldn't just let his goon kill Josh and kidnap her.

"Now, Deputy, drop your gun, or the next shot goes into her. It won't kill her, but it'll put her in enough pain to make you wish you'd cooperated."

She looked back at Josh. Didn't see surrender in his eyes. She saw only determination to end this. But he dropped his gun. It fell on the ground just a few inches from her feet.

Jaycee glanced around the woods, but didn't see Gage or anyone else who could help them. She hoped he was nearby and hearing all of this so he could maybe ambush the gunman. After all, this goon was just one man, and Josh had killed the other one who'd been behind them.

Of course, there could be others in the car.

Her stomach knotted.

Because there might be more than one other kidnapper. With all their attempts to kidnap her, Jaycee wouldn't be surprised if the whole car was filled with guards ready to haul her off to a baby farm.

"So what now?" Jaycee demanded from the kidnapper. She hiked up her chin and tried to sound a lot tougher and stronger than she felt.

"We wait for a few minutes until the road is clear so we can leave."

She prayed that didn't mean one of the guards had found Gage, but she figured if they'd set up a plan like this, then they would have brought enough reinforcements.

"In the meantime, the deputy puts down his gun, steps aside and you come with us," the gunman continued. "If you don't make a fuss, the deputy lives."

She swallowed hard. Jaycee didn't believe him for one second. No way would he allow Josh to live, because they'd both seen his face. Still, she wanted to do something—anything—to save Josh.

But what?

There were a lot of options here, and she couldn't count on Gage and the others arriving in time.

"I'll come with you if you bring Josh, too," she blurted out.

Her offer wasn't well received.

Josh cursed. "What the hell do you think you're doing?"

The goon just stared at her as if she'd lost her mind. "If this is some kind of trick," he said, "it's a dangerous one."

Maybe, but Josh and she stood a better chance of surviving if they were together in the car, preferably with her in front of him so the goon couldn't shoot him again.

She couldn't be sure, but she thought the kidnapper smiled. "Admirable, trying to save your boyfriend, but it won't work if he doesn't cooperate." He turned his head slightly and mumbled something. To the person in the car no doubt. "Okay. Time to move."

Neither Jaycee nor Josh budged. "Whatever your buyer's paying for the baby, I'll double it," Josh fired back.

If the offer surprised the man, he didn't show any signs of it. And he definitely didn't step out from cover. "Oh, you'll get the chance to do that when the baby's born and if you're still alive then."

So this was about selling the baby and maybe didn't have anything to do with her being an FBI agent. And if the man was telling the truth, they did indeed have a buyer.

A thought that sickened her.

Someone was out there and wanted to buy her baby as if it were cattle.

"The being alive part is up to you," the man said to

Josh. "It's simple. Cooperate now and you live. Don't co-operate and you die."

"Let's walk toward the car," she whispered to Josh.

However, it went against all her FBI training to actually get in the car. Because the stats were that once these goons had control over Josh and her, things would only get worse. But there were a lot of steps between the car and them.

Those steps could be their chance to escape.

Escape how exactly, she didn't know, but it was clear this goon wasn't going to give them much more time.

Jaycee took the first of those steps but then stopped when she heard the sound.

Gunfire.

Not behind them where Josh had shot the kidnapper and where she'd last seen Grayson. This was coming from their right. Where Gage would likely be.

Again, the kidnapper didn't seem surprised. Nor did he even glance in that direction. He kept his attention pinned to Josh and her, and he aimed his gun at Jaycee.

"Move now, Deputy, or I shoot her in the arm just like I did you. I'm pretty sure blood loss wouldn't be good for that baby she's carrying."

Jaycee took another step and Josh followed. Putting him closer to his gun that he'd dropped on the ground. If she dived to the side, maybe Josh could get his gun and get off a shot. It wouldn't be an easy one with the moron crouched behind the door, but it might be the only chance they had.

The gunshots stopped, and she said another prayer. That Gage had won that round. It was impossible to tell because the kidnapper didn't have a reaction to that, either. He simply used his gun to motion for her to keep moving.

One more step.

Josh, too. And he stopped.

His boot was right next to the gun.

"Drop now," Josh whispered to her.

Jaycee was about to do that to give Josh a chance to take out the kidnapper, but she froze when she heard the sound to her right. The person was walking straight toward them.

Not Gage.

However, it was someone Jaycee recognized.

And the person was pointing a gun right at Josh.

Sierra.

Josh wasn't sure who would be on the other end of that gun, but he'd figured it would be Bryson. Or Valerie. He hadn't expected Sierra, since it'd been less than twenty-four hours since she'd given birth to her daughter.

This was hardly the place for a new mother.

Or a mother-to-be.

He had to get Jaycee out of there, but how? It was hard to think with the pain stabbing in his arm. Yeah, it was just a flesh wound, but that didn't stop it from hurting like crazy and dulling his mind.

Sierra kept the gun on Josh, and after blowing out a weary, tired breath, she opened the back door of the car and sank down on the seat, facing outward and with her feet still on the ground. She did not look like a happy camper when she glanced over at the kidnapper.

Correction: her minion.

It was clear who was in charge here, and Sierra was definitely the boss.

"You just couldn't get this done yourself, huh?" she snarled at the guy. "Made me walk all the way over here from the other car. You know how hard it is to push out a kid?" She didn't wait for an answer. "Damn hard, and I expect you to pick up the slack while I'm recovering."

"What do you want me to do, boss?" the man jumped to ask.

"Well, now we have to wait, don't we? No doubt thanks to one of his badge-wearing cousins." She shot Josh a glare. "Someone disabled the vehicle we used to block the road so no one else could drive in and get to me. I'm guessing it was a Ryland lawman who did that."

That was Josh's guess, too, and he was glad one of them had managed to do that.

"You shot the person?" Jaycee asked, her voice trembling now. It was exactly what Josh had planned to ask.

"Of course. I killed him." Sierra added a taunting smile.

Josh didn't put much stock in the answer or the smile. "Liar. If you'd killed him, you wouldn't be worried about being ambushed right now. You wouldn't be cowering in the car."

That put some venom in her eyes that even the darkness couldn't hide. "If you think you're going to goad me into standing out in the open, think again, cowboy. I'm not stupid, and just because I took care of one Ryland, that doesn't mean there aren't others out and about."

There were. Or at least there should be. By now, Grayson would have alerted the entire family, and they'd be combing the woods looking for Jaycee and him.

"Of course, the fires we set will keep them occupied for a while," Sierra added a heartbeat later.

"What fires?" Josh lifted his head, hoping this was yet another lie, but then he silently cursed. Because he did indeed smell some smoke.

What the hell had she done now?

"We set a few fires in the barns and near the houses," she happily explained. "They were on timers, so you probably didn't get a glimpse of them before you came running out to save Jaycee."

He hadn't, but Josh didn't think she was lying about this. "If you hurt my family, you're a dead woman."

Sierra laughed, a short burst of laughter that had no humor in it. "You Rylands breed like rabbits," she added in a grumble. "Too bad you're not all women because you'd make nice additions to my little cottage industry."

So that's what she was calling it. "Cottage industry is tame sounding for what's really multiple felonies," Josh accused her. "How many people have you murdered, Sierra?"

"Enough that you should be worried about me holding this gun on you," she continued, sounding pleased with herself now. "All I want to do is finish this up and get a good night's sleep. And that'll happen. Once that car's out of the way, we're leaving."

Josh figured it wouldn't be easy to move a car on such a narrow road. No place to put it because of the trees and the ditches. Sierra's plan to keep anyone else from using the road had backfired. He hoped the rest of her plan did, too.

"What'd you do with your baby?" Jaycee asked. "Did you sell her, too?"

If Sierra was insulted by that, she didn't show it. She just lifted her shoulder in a careless shrug. "She's with the nanny, along with some other soon-to-be mothers. She's all tucked away safe and sound, waiting for Bryson to pay through the nose if he wants an heir as much as he claims he does."

So her daughter was likely at a baby farm. Too bad Sierra hadn't spilled the location, but he might be able to get that out of her if she kept talking.

"But Bryson's not the father of your baby," Josh tossed out there. "Blood tests prove it."

Again, she just shrugged. "Blood tests, like everything else, can be faked. Bryson wants to believe this child is his. Or maybe it's not even that. Maybe he just wants an heir and doesn't care about the test results."

Sad, but true. Bryson was all about the money. Still,

the man had seemed plenty upset that Sierra was trying to extort money from him.

"Bryson got himself into a bad fix," Sierra went on. "He owes money to the wrong people. Loan sharks. So what did he do? He borrowed more money from even worse people to pay his debts. I figure right about now, he'll do anything to get an heir so he can claim his inheritance."

"I'm guessing you'll be more than willing to take some of that inheritance from him," Jaycee muttered, sarcasm dripping from her voice.

"Seems only fair that I get half." In Sierra's warped, money-hungry mind, that probably did seem fair.

Josh's phone buzzed, but it was in Jaycee's pocket so he couldn't see it.

"Uh-uh," Sierra warned Jaycee when she reached for it. "Keep your hands where I can see them." She glanced over her shoulder. "Find out what the hell's taking so long with that car. I want out of here now."

Josh got a glimpse of the person she was speaking to. Not Bryson or Valerie, but Josh was pretty sure it was one of the guards who'd escaped from the baby farm raid. The one who'd shoved Jaycee into the barn. The man took out a phone and made a call.

Jaycee adjusted her position just a little and just enough so that she was no longer in the way of him getting his gun. Now all he needed was some kind of distraction. Too bad he couldn't let Grayson know that. But then, Grayson might be too occupied with the fires to do much of anything right now.

"Quit moving," Sierra snapped. "You're making me antsy with that fidgeting."

"What about your sister and Bryson?" Jaycee asked, obviously not addressing the moving issue. Which she did again. Just a fraction to the side. So that she wouldn't be in Josh's line of fire. "Are they in on this with you?"

"Please, I don't need help running this operation. Bryson's an idiot, and Valerie's too busy bad-mouthing me to help me. However, my sister did fund the start-up of my business."

"With or without her knowledge?" Jaycee fired back.

"Without," Sierra readily admitted. "Valerie wouldn't knowingly help me do anything that would get me ahead in life."

Well, that was something at least, and Josh thought Sierra was telling the truth. About this anyway. "How did you milk the money from her?" Josh asked. "Did you just come out and steal it?"

There it was again. That flash of anger in her eyes. Maybe Sierra didn't like being called a common thief. Well, she was a thief, all right, but not of the common variety. It'd taken a lot of money and brains to put together an operation like this.

"I didn't steal it," Sierra snapped. "I cut a deal with one of her longtime employees. Someone she trusted but who was in desperate need of cash. He lied to Valerie, saying he needed lots of cash for medical treatments. I had the medical records faked, and the employee and I split the money."

That explained the withdrawals from Valerie's bank account. It didn't, however, explain plenty of other things about the baby farms. Josh wanted those answers, but he wanted to get them with Sierra handcuffed and on her way to jail.

"About five more minutes," her hired gun relayed to Sierra when he got off the phone.

Josh saw the man's guns then. All three were armed with multiple weapons, and that wasn't good odds for him. Still, he had to do something, and five minutes wasn't much time. His best shot was probably when one of them got behind the wheel. Of course, by then they'd be trying to force Jaycee into the car.

"Come on," Sierra said, her voice taunting again. She looked at Jaycee. "You don't want to ask me why you were kidnapped?"

"I figured you'd tell me when you were ready." Jaycee sounded about as happy with this conversation as Josh was. He hoped he could use every bit of info Sierra was gushing about to put the woman away for life. Of course, for that to happen, Jaycee and he had to get out of there alive.

"Guess I'm ready." Sierra smiled. "I have a buyer who can't father his own children, but he had a very interesting shopping list when it came to baby characteristics. Your eye and hair color but with some criminal DNA so he could train the kid to follow in his footsteps. Perfect match. You might wear a badge, Agent Finney, but your mama and daddy were lifers in prison. That appealed to him."

Jaycee made a soft moan. It was torture listening to this and imagining their precious baby being handed over to a slimeball criminal.

"And what about Miranda Culley?" Josh asked. He didn't really want to know, but he had to stop Sierra from talking about his baby. Because if she said one more word about it, he might just pick up his gun and risk being shot so he could put some bullets in her.

"The woman didn't even know about what was going on. I picked her name from the missing persons registry on the internet. Figured she'd be the perfect front to lure you to the cemetery so I could take Jaycee."

"But you failed." Josh took pleasure in reminding her of that.

"Yes, that time I did because doofus here got the car bogged down on a dirt road." She tipped her head to the man behind the door and motioned for him to get behind the wheel. "I didn't want the Ryland clan combing the woods and maybe coming up on that car, so I faked the injury. It hurt like hell, too."

Sierra touched the spot on her forehead, smiled at Josh when her gaze dropped to his arm. Then his chest. "But you know a little about hurt and pain, don't you, Deputy Ryland? Just how bad are those flashbacks from your PTSD?"

Suddenly, they weren't bad at all.

In fact, Josh's head was pretty damn clear. Especially now that one of the minions had his back to him.

"Get down," Josh warned Jaycee, and in the same breath, he snatched up his gun.

Josh was the first to pull the trigger.

THE SHOTS BLASTED through the air, punctuated by Sierra's screams and sounds of pain, and Jaycee had no choice but to dive for cover. Unarmed, she couldn't help Josh, but she could hope and pray that they both got out of the path of those bullets.

Jaycee got behind the tree trunk again, and when she looked in the direction of the car, the driver was slumped on the ground. Josh had taken cover, too. Well, of sorts. He was behind a small tree that didn't fully protect his body.

"You bastard!" Sierra yelled. "You'll pay for that." And she snatched the gun from the guard who was on the backseat with her.

She fired, despite the fact the man was trying to get the gun back.

Jaycee's breath stalled in her throat, and she started praying again. It must have worked, because Sierra's shot didn't come anywhere near close to Josh. Of course, any shot fired right now could hit one of Josh's cousins. She figured there were plenty of them in the woods and maybe on the road trying to figure a way to stop this.

"Give me the gun," the man in the car said. Not an order because he was obviously talking to his boss, but he was clearly pleading with her.

Sierra ignored him. Cursing, she fired again.

So did Josh.

Sierra missed. Josh didn't.

Josh's shot slammed into Sierra's shoulder and she screamed again. Cursed him, too. What she didn't do was let go of the gun despite the blood that was seeping through her blouse. However, the man pulled her all the way inside the car and shut the door.

"We need Sierra to keep alive," Josh called out.

Yes, they did. Because she was the only person who could tell them the extent of the baby farms. They didn't even know how many there were and where they were located, and they could pressure Sierra to help them save the women and their babies.

With the door closed and both Sierra and one gunman still alive, Josh stayed down but maneuvered himself closer to the car.

Jaycee had lost count of how many bullets Josh had left. He had his Glock, which meant he'd started with twenty-two bullets. Not a lot considering the gunfight they'd been in since the kidnappers had dragged her away from Josh's place.

Sierra was still cursing and howling in pain, but Jaycee saw some movement in the car.

No.

The remaining guard was climbing over the seat to get behind the wheel. If that happened, they might escape. Jaycee didn't want Josh or his family to take any more risks, but she didn't want Sierra getting away, either.

Josh moved closer at the same time the car engine started. The driver rolled forward, pushing the dead gunman out of the way. If he managed to get the door shut, Josh wouldn't be able to fire inside. Not with that bullet-proof glass in the way.

"Jaycee, watch out!" someone yelled.

It took her a moment to realize that it wasn't Josh, but rather Grayson. She turned around and didn't see Grayson, but she saw something that put her heart right in her throat.

The armed man running toward her.

He lifted his gun, aiming not at her but at Josh. Josh turned, too, his gaze snagging the guy, and he dropped to the ground.

And Josh and the guard fired at the same time.

Jaycee was afraid to look. Terrified that the bullet might have killed Josh.

But he was fine.

Unfortunately, so was the other guy, and he fired another shot as he ducked behind one of the trees. She was beyond thankful that Josh hadn't been shot again, but that didn't stop the car from moving.

Sierra was getting away.

"Everyone get down!" she heard Gage yell.

She dropped all the way to the ground and prayed that Josh and Grayson did the same. A split second later, the shots started. Not coming from the side of the car where they were but from the other side.

Gage, no doubt.

He just started shooting, and unlike Josh, it didn't sound as if he'd run out of ammo. The bullets pelted against the glass, and judging from Sierra's screams, some of them got through.

She saw Josh lift his head, take aim, and he shot out the

two tires on their side. The car bobbed to a stop, the flat rubber unable to get enough traction on the dirt.

Jaycee blew out a quick breath of relief. But there was no relief when she saw both car doors fly open. Sierra and her henchmen didn't get out of the vehicle, but still using the protective glass in the car, they took aim.

The man aimed at Josh.

Sierra, at Jaycee.

The shots tore into the fallen tree, chipping away huge chunks of the wood. Jaycee saw Josh dive back to the ground, and she could hear shots from the direction where she'd last heard Grayson. The only armed one who wasn't firing was Gage, and she soon caught sight of him.

He was on the other side of the car.

And he joined the gunfire. This time at much closer range, and even though Jaycee couldn't see it, she figured his shots had to be chipping away at the glass.

"Stop!" Sierra yelled. "We're surrendering."

Gage, Grayson and Josh all stopped, and eerie silence settled over the road and woods.

Jaycee couldn't believe Sierra would surrender, but maybe she was smart enough to realize it was the only way she was going to make it out alive. So she could then escape. No way would a woman like Sierra go to jail, and unfortunately, she had plenty of henchmen in place to make sure that didn't happen.

The gunman stepped from the car slowly, dropping his weapon on the ground and lifting his hands in the air. The seconds crawled by, all of them waiting for Sierra to do the same.

But she didn't.

Screaming like someone crazy, Sierra came out, a gun in each hand, and she started shooting.

"You're a dead woman, Jaycee!" she yelled, and she took aim at Jaycee's head.

However, Sierra never got a chance to pull the trigger. Josh's shots saw to that. This time, he didn't aim for her arm. He couldn't because he had to stop her from killing Jaycee. When the bullet hit her chest, Sierra froze, her eyes wide with shock.

Then, nothing.

Her guns slid from her hands, and she crumpled onto the ground.

Jaycee and Josh started running toward the woman at the same time. Josh got there first and touched his fingers to Sierra's neck.

"Call an ambulance," Josh yelled. "She's alive."

Chapter Twenty

Josh tried not to wince or react when the nurse stitched up his arm. Jaycee was no doubt already feeling enough stress without his bad reaction adding to it. With the eagle-eyed way she was watching him, it would definitely add stress if she thought he was in pain.

"You sure you're okay?" Jaycee asked, and it was something she'd asked a lot on the drive to the Silver Creek hospital and since they'd arrived.

Yeah, despite the throbbing from the gunshot wound and the stitches, he was fine, even better now that the doctor had said Jaycee was all right. Josh hadn't let the doctor check him out until he knew all was well with her and the baby.

Sierra was a different matter.

She'd been alive when the ambulance had finally managed to get into that remote part of the ranch, and she was now in surgery. However, Dr. Mickelson had warned them that while Sierra's chances looked good, she still might not survive.

And Josh blamed himself for that.

He'd had no choice but to shoot her, or Sierra would have gunned down Jaycee. Josh had tried not to go for a kill shot, but that had been hard to do, especially since Sierra hadn't been standing still. Instead, the woman had let the rage take over and had been trying to get into a better position to end Jaycee's life.

Now he could only hope for the best.

In this case, the best was for Sierra to stay alive at least long enough to lead them to the baby farms and her own daughter. Josh was hoping and praying they could get that info by some other means, but it was sad but true that Sierra might be their only chance at doing that.

The nurse finally finished with him, and Josh stood, pulling down his sleeve so that Jaycee wouldn't have to see the stitches. Of course, that meant she could see the blood on his shirt.

She saw it, all right.

Tears welled in her eyes, and she pulled him into a gentle hug. "I'm so sorry."

Jaycee made it sound as if all of this was her fault. It wasn't. She'd been a victim, and if Sierra and her minions had had their way, Jaycee would have soon been a dead victim. After she'd delivered the baby who would be sold to some slimeball criminal, that was.

Sierra's heart had to be as black as night to have made an arrangement like that.

"Don't let it eat away at you," Jaycee whispered, as if she knew exactly what he was thinking. It was spooky just how often they were on the same wavelength.

Josh brushed a kiss on her cheek. Didn't dare risk more. His body was one big giant nerve right now, and if he really kissed her, he might not stop. Because right now, having Jaycee in his arms melted away the pain. The memories.

And even the nightmare that'd just happened.

As she'd said, he wouldn't let it eat away at him, but that was because he had Jaycee there to remind him that there was another side of life. A good one that didn't involve kidnappers and baby farms.

Josh kept his arm around Jaycee's waist as they left the examining room and went back into the waiting area. In this case, it was aptly named since there were two people waiting for them.

Grayson and Valerie.

The person missing was his brother, Sawyer, who'd been there earlier, not long after Josh and the others had arrived.

Valerie immediately got to her feet. "How's Sierra?"

Josh had to shake his head. "She's still in surgery." And she might be there for a while. That was a best-case scenario because it would mean she was not only still alive but also that the damage was being repaired. "The doctor expects her to live."

Valerie's legs buckled, and she dropped back down into the chair. "Good. I know you don't think much of her, but she's still my sister."

Josh could understand that. In part. He would be devastated if something happened to his brother. But then, Sawyer wasn't an insane criminal who'd wrecked heaven knows how many lives for the sake of money.

Grayson stood, blowing out a long, weary breath, and he studied both Jaycee and Josh. "Are you two really okay?"

Josh waited for Jaycee to nod before he added one of his own. He figured it'd be a while, though, before it was actually the truth, since both of them had come damn close to dying tonight, and they could thank Sierra and her henchmen for that.

Josh tipped his head to the empty seat where he'd last seen his brother. "Where's Sawyer?"

"Out looking for the baby farm and Sierra's daughter. Gage found two recent addresses on the GPS in the car Sierra was using."

That was the best news Josh had heard all day. Well,

other than hearing from the doctor that Jaycee and the baby were okay. "Sawyer and Gage are checking them out now," Grayson added.

"Not alone?" Jaycee immediately said.

Grayson shook his head. "Kade and some other FBI agents went with them." He glanced down at the phone in his hand. "I'm hoping for a call from them any minute."

Josh hoped that call would be good news. He was sick and tired of hearing mostly bad stuff when it came to this. Plus, if this turned out to be the locations of the baby farms, they wouldn't need to wait for Sierra to come out of surgery and then recovery. They could go in and rescue the captives.

"When Sierra's baby is found," Valerie said, getting to her feet again, "I'll take her." She stopped, sucked in a quick breath. Blinked back tears, too. "She's my niece, and I love her. I swear, I'd do my best to take care of her."

She sounded sincere enough, and heck, maybe she was. Josh had been dealing with scum for so long that it was hard to see the good in people.

"When the baby's found," Josh started. And he used *when* instead of *if* because he refused to believe the little girl would just disappear in this baby farm maze. "We'll get it all sorted out. You're the next of kin so you'll have a big say in what happens to her."

Valerie gave a shaky nod and sank back down onto the chair. "And when Sierra recovers from her injuries, she'll be going to jail."

For a long, long time. They were all thinking it, but none of them said it aloud. Judging from Sierra's behavior tonight, she had likely even committed murder, and that could get her the death penalty.

Ironic that she would survive a gunshot only to face

that. But Josh had no sympathy for the woman who'd destroyed and tried to destroy so many lives.

Including his and Jaycee's.

"You should take Jaycee back to the ranch," Grayson suggested. "Not to your place but mine or the main house. It'll take a while to clear out the smell of the tear gas in your apartment."

Yeah, it would, but thankfully that was the only damage. Josh had been worried about the fires that Sierra had claimed had been set. And a few had been. But Grayson had already told him that the ranch hands had easily contained them, and there'd been no real damage. Sierra had only meant the fires to be a distraction.

They'd worked, in part.

The fires had tied up some of his cousins and the ranch hands. But that hadn't stopped Gage, Grayson, Jaycee and him from stopping Sierra.

"Did you figure out how the kidnappers got on the ranch?" Jaycee asked.

Grayson lifted his shoulder. "Probably came in with the wedding decorators. Dad tried to check everyone's IDs, but there were a lot of people coming and going. He thinks they might have sneaked in one of the vans that were bringing in supplies."

"This wasn't his fault," Jaycee said. "Sierra was determined to kidnap me. Sooner or later, she would have found a way to get to me."

It was the truth, and it hurt Josh far more than a gunshot wound. No matter what precautions they'd taken, Sierra and her goons had figured out a way around them. But that was over now. Sierra and her hired guns would go to jail for the rest of their lives.

"I'll call you with any updates," Grayson added, and he handed Josh the keys to his truck. "Dade and Bree are waiting outside to go with you."

"Oh, God," Jaycee mumbled, and he knew why she'd said that.

Because the danger maybe wasn't over.

That was the reason Grayson had arranged for Bree and Dade to ride with them. They were protection that they might end up needing. Again.

"It'll be okay," Josh whispered to her, and he got her moving toward the exit. "Soon we'll put all of this behind us, and you can focus on having a healthy baby."

That was his wish list anyway. Now he had to make it happen.

However, Jaycee stopped and faced him. "It will be okay," she said, surprising him.

After everything that'd just happened, he expected at least a little bit of gloom and doom, but she slid her hand over her stomach. And kissed him.

"You saved my life tonight. Multiple times. Thank you for that," she said.

You're welcome didn't seem nearly heartfelt enough. "You saved me a couple of times, too."

She nodded, and Josh leaned in for another kiss, but she pressed her hand over his mouth. "I'm just going to say this fast. Like ripping off a bandage. I'm in love with you, and I know that's not the right thing to say. That it puts a lot of pressure on you—"

Josh moved her hand away and kissed her. It wasn't to shut her up.

Okay, that was part of it.

He just figured the best way to shut her up was to re-mind her of this heat that was between them.

And it was a reminder, all right.

He kissed her until air became a serious issue, and they had to break away to catch their breaths.

"I tell you I love you, and that's how you react?" Jaycee frowned, shook her head. "Wait, that didn't come out right. What I meant—"

He kissed her again. "I know what you meant," he whispered against her mouth. "You want to know how I feel about that? Well, I don't feel pressured, that's for sure, and it was the absolute right thing to say. Because I'm in love with you, too."

Until that moment he hadn't known for sure, but it was true. He was crazy, head over heels in love with Jaycee. He wasn't sure when or where it'd happened, but he was certain of his feelings for her.

She smiled. Then it faded, and she got another of those concerned looks in her eyes. "But what about the past?"

"It's the past," he quickly let her know, and he put his hand on her stomach. "Seems best for us to focus on the future now."

Despite everything he'd just told her, her concerned look went up a significant notch. "You're not in love with me just because of the baby?"

"No." And that was yet something else he knew with absolute certainty.

Josh would have proved that with another kiss, but he heard Grayson's phone ring, and both Jaycee and he turned back around to see if this was good news.

Or if they truly did need protection driving to the ranch.

"Gage," Grayson said.

Josh couldn't hear a word Gage said, and he couldn't tell from Grayson's expression, either. All he could do was stand there and wait to find out what was going on.

And take care of some much-needed personal stuff.

"Marry me," he whispered to Jaycee.

She didn't move. Didn't respond. She certainly didn't jump into his arms and say yes. And that meant he'd blown this big-time. He should have guessed after her reaction to his last marriage proposal. Of course, that one hadn't been the real deal.

This one was.

"I'm not asking you to marry me because of the baby," he quickly clarified. "Though that's a nice bonus. But the reason I proposed is because I'm in love with you and I want to spend the rest of my life with you."

Jaycee still didn't move, but tears welled in her eyes, and she made a little gasping sound.

"Oh, man." Josh groaned. "Now I've made you cry."

"For the best of reasons," she said.

Her voice was all warmth and breath now, and there was no more concern in her expression. She put her arms around him and kissed him until Josh was feeling all warm and breathy, too.

Actually, he was wishing he could haul her off to bed. And he figured soon he could make that happen.

"Yes," she whispered.

Because he was caught up in the kiss, it took him a moment to realize that was the best thing Jaycee could have said to him.

"Yes?" he clarified and hoped like the devil that he hadn't misunderstood.

He hadn't. Her slow smile and quick nod proved that. So did their next kiss, and it went on a little longer than planned because he heard Grayson clear his throat.

"Sounds as if congratulations are in order," Grayson said, smiling. "Well, I can give you two something else to celebrate. You, too," he said to Valerie. "They found both of the baby farms, and Sierra's daughter was at one of them."

While that sounded good, Josh immediately thought of the guards who'd escaped with those women. "Did Gage say if there were any injuries or escapees?"

"Doesn't appear to be. There were four women at the first place. Three more at the second, and those women are the ones who were taken from the farm where Jaycee had been held."

"And they're okay?" Jaycee asked.

Grayson nodded. "Everyone is okay, and the guards have been arrested."

Jaycee made a sound of sheer relief and landed in his arms again.

"Are the guards talking?" Josh asked. Because they might need info from them to find any other baby farms that Sierra had set up.

"One's talking, and that's all it takes. We'll cut a deal with him so he can testify against the others. And against Sierra. He's already told Kade that he'll spill any- and everything."

That was definitely a huge reason to celebrate. Of course, the guard might not know the full extent of Sierra's operation, but Josh wasn't going to borrow trouble. What the guard didn't know they could probably piece together with the other evidence they'd find at the baby farm locations.

Plus, there was Sierra.

When she came out of surgery, she might be willing to give information to take the death penalty off the table. Sierra was the sort of woman who'd do all sorts of bargaining to stay alive, and that in turn could save anyone else who was unlucky enough to have been kidnapped and held.

"I'll wait here until Sierra's out of surgery," Grayson added. "When she wakes up, I'll let you know."

Josh thanked him and got Jaycee moving toward the door again. It seemed odd, stepping outside without worrying if someone was going to try to kidnap or kill them. It felt like a new lease on life.

Which it was.

He was in love with Jaycee, and she was in love with him. Yeah, definitely a new lease.

"So how will this work?" she asked, looping her arm around his waist. "Will we live at the ranch after we're married?"

"I'd like that. But if there are too many bad memories—"

"There are good memories, too," she interrupted. "Like before the kidnappers came."

Yeah, making love to Jaycee was indeed a good memory, and he hoped to create a lot more memories just like that one. In bed and out.

"Don't know if your place will be big enough, though, when the baby comes," she continued.

"So we can build a place like Grayson's. There's plenty of land, and it might be fun to see our baby playing with all the cousins."

"Our baby," she repeated and stopped again. "So when we build this house, what color are we painting the nursery?"

"Green," he teased. "It's my favorite color."

She gave him a playful jab in the stomach. "Pink or blue?"

"Both."

Jaycee blinked. And Josh laughed. "Blue this time. But I'm hoping next time, we can go for pink."

Josh kissed that smile right off Jaycee's mouth, scooped her up and started for home.

Oh, yeah, there'd definitely be a next time.

* * * * *

Don't miss USA TODAY *bestselling author*
Delores Fossen's next book in her miniseries
THE LAWMEN OF SILVER CREEK RANCH.
Look for SAWYER next month,
wherever Harlequin Intrigue books are sold!

REQUEST YOUR FREE BOOKS!
2 FREE NOVELS PLUS 2 FREE GIFTS!

HARLEQUIN

INTRIGUE

BREATHTAKING ROMANTIC SUSPENSE

YES! Please send me 2 FREE Harlequin Intrigue® novels and my 2 FREE gifts (gifts are worth about $10). After receiving them, if I don't wish to receive any more books, I can return the shipping statement marked "cancel." If I don't cancel, I will receive 6 brand-new novels every month and be billed just $4.74 per book in the U.S. or $5.24 per book in Canada. That's a savings of at least 14% off the cover price! It's quite a bargain! Shipping and handling is just 50¢ per book in the U.S. and 75¢ per book in Canada.* I understand that accepting the 2 free books and gifts places me under no obligation to buy anything. I can always return a shipment and cancel at any time. Even if I never buy another book, the two free books and gifts are mine to keep forever.

182/382 HDN F42N

Name	(PLEASE PRINT)
Address	Apt. #
City	State/Prov.	Zip/Postal Code

Signature (if under 18, a parent or guardian must sign)

Mail to the Harlequin® Reader Service:
IN U.S.A.: P.O. Box 1867, Buffalo, NY 14240-1867
IN CANADA: P.O. Box 609, Fort Erie, Ontario L2A 5X3
Are you a subscriber to Harlequin Intrigue books
and want to receive the larger-print edition?
Call 1-800-873-8635 or visit www.ReaderService.com.

* Terms and prices subject to change without notice. Prices do not include applicable taxes. Sales tax applicable in N.Y. Canadian residents will be charged applicable taxes. Offer not valid in Quebec. This offer is limited to one order per household. Not valid for current subscribers to Harlequin Intrigue books. All orders subject to credit approval. Credit or debit balances in a customer's account(s) may be offset by any other outstanding balance owed by or to the customer. Please allow 4 to 6 weeks for delivery. Offer available while quantities last.

Your Privacy—The Harlequin® Reader Service is committed to protecting your privacy. Our Privacy Policy is available online at www.ReaderService.com or upon request from the Harlequin Reader Service.

We make a portion of our mailing list available to reputable third parties that offer products we believe may interest you. If you prefer that we not exchange your name with third parties, or if you wish to clarify or modify your communication preferences, please visit us at www.ReaderService.com/consumerchoice or write to us at Harlequin Reader Service Preference Service, P.O. Box 9062, Buffalo, NY 14269. Include your complete name and address.

HI13R

SAWYER
by USA TODAY *bestselling author*
Delores Fossen

*A woman he'd spent one incredible night with and the
baby who could be his will have Agent Sawyer Ryland
fighting for a future he never imagined...*

Agent Sawyer Ryland caught the movement from the corner
of his eye, turned and saw the blonde pushing her way through
the other guests who'd gathered for the wedding reception.

She wasn't hard to spot.

She was practically running, and she had a bundle of
something gripped in front of her like a shield.

Sawyer's pulse kicked up a notch, and he automatically
slid his hand inside his jacket and over his Glock. It was sad
that his first response was to pull his firearm even at his own
brother's wedding reception. Still, he'd been an FBI agent
long enough—and had been shot too many times—that he
lived by the code of better safe than sorry.

Or better safe than dead.

She stopped in the center of the barn that'd been deco-
rated with hundreds of clear twinkling lights and flowers,
and even though she was wearing dark sunglasses, Sawyer
was pretty sure that her gaze rifled around. Obviously looking for someone. However, the looking around skidded to a
halt when her attention landed on him.

"Sawyer," she said.

HIEXP69758

Because of the chattering guests and the fiddler sawing out some bluegrass, Sawyer didn't actually hear her speak his name. Instead, he saw it shape her trembling mouth. She yanked off the sunglasses, her gaze colliding with his.

"Cassidy O'Neal," he mumbled.

Yeah, it was her all right. Except she didn't much look like a pampered princess doll today in her jeans and body-swallowing gray T-shirt.

Despite the fact that he wasn't giving off any welcoming vibes whatsoever, Cassidy hurried to him. Her mouth was still trembling. Her dark green eyes rapidly blinking. There were beads of sweat on her forehead and upper lip despite the half dozen or so massive fans circulating air into the barn.

"I'm sorry," she said, and she thrust whatever she was carrying at him.

Sawyer didn't take it and backed up, but not before he caught a glimpse of the tiny hand gripping the white blanket.

A baby.

That put his heart right in his suddenly dry throat.

To find out what happens,
don't miss USA TODAY *bestselling author*
Delores Fossen's SAWYER, on sale in May 2014,
wherever Harlequin® Intrigue® books are sold!

HIEXP69758